Elizabeth eyed Price derisively. 'You might put up a respectable façade, Mr Domenico, but underneath it all you wangle things your way by whatever means you've set up for your purpose. Favours swapped for favours under the table. Isn't that how it goes? I mean, with your father... being what he was...'

Suddenly, she couldn't go on. Hearing her own words—it was so distasteful, alien to everything she had ever lived by. Shock at her own madness paralysed her mind.

A cold, bleak look settled on Price Domenico's face. He sagged back in his chair, his whole body expressing weary defeat. His mouth twisted into a savage little grimace. Then he looked up at her and the mockery was back in his eyes.

'Tell me, Miss Kent. How much can you afford... for your brand of justice?'

Books you will enjoy
by EMMA DARCY

THE ALOHA BRIDE

Robyn's encounter with Julian Lassiter came at a low point in her life—which was partly why she found herself wanting to solve his problems, in a way that was not merely reckless, but positively dangerous!

THE ULTIMATE CHOICE

The new owner of Marian Park was an arrogant swine who wanted to ruin Kelly's show-jumping career. But she wouldn't be stopped—even if she had to confront Justin St John with all guns blazing...

THE POWER AND THE PASSION

Bernadette's father warned her to steer clear of the dark, disturbing tycoon, Danton Fayette—but some deep instinct in her rose to meet the challenge. She was determined to prove her father wrong—but knew she would have to fight her attraction to Danton all the way...

TOO STRONG TO DENY

BY

EMMA DARCY

MILLS & BOON LIMITED
ETON HOUSE 18-24 PARADISE ROAD
RICHMOND SURREY TW9 1SR

First published in Great Britain 1990
by Mills & Boon Limited

This edition 1990

ISBN 0 263 76584 9

Set in Times Roman 11 on 12 pt.
01-9003-50309 C

Made and printed in Great Britain

CHAPTER ONE

ELIZABETH might not have gone to see Price Domenico, except for the comment made by the solicitor she had consulted.

He had said she was stupid!

He had even gone beyond that. He'd said that going to see Price Domenico was the most stupid thing he had ever heard of.

Elizabeth's ire had already been raised to firing point by the advice he had given her. She had contained her outrage, silently seething behind her disciplined dignity, but no amount of self-discipline could tackle that remark and come out on top.

It was like waving a red rag at a bull.

Elizabeth charged at it.

There was no other remark the solicitor could have made which she would have found so inflammatory. Except perhaps calling the Royal Family by their first names. Elizabeth had been named after Her Majesty The Queen. But she had never measured up. Not by her father's rigorous standards.

Her father had been a commander in the navy. He had been wounded in the face during the Korean War, and maybe that had soured his life. Or maybe any softness in him had died with his young wife. If Elizabeth had ever been loved by her father, he had certainly had a contrary way of showing it. All she could remember was savage discipline.

If she did anything wrong—broke a cup or a plate, or failed to notice a button missing from his clothes—anything at all—he would drag her up before him, stand her to attention, and tell her eye to eye that she was stupid.

And then there had been her husband, the man who had seemed so wonderfully loving—before they got married. He had called her stupid, too. It had seemed at the time, that she had leapt out of the frying-pan into the fire, exchanging one tyrant for another. But that was well in the past now. She had reverted to her maiden name, unwilling to keep any tie with the man she had married in blind good faith.

Her father had gone first, dying of a heart attack. Then her husband—despite his arrogant belief that he could survive any reckless risk at all—proved himself as mortal as anyone else by hurtling to his death in his beloved speedboat. His last words to Elizabeth had been that she was stupid for not sharing his mad love of speed.

It hadn't been easy, sticking to a sense of self-worth. She wasn't the most gifted student in the world, but she did have application. She almost had her Bachelor of Arts degree now—would receive it at the end of the year, if all went well. Five years of hard slog—teaching during the day to earn her living, and studying at night as an external student of the New England University at Armidale—but the achievement was worth it.

Since the demise of the two men who had stamped their opinion all over her, Elizabeth had set out to prove one thing—the one thing that was more important than anything else. That she was not stupid! Once she had that piece of paper in her hands—Bachelor of Arts—she could wave it under the nose of anyone who dared to suggest she was lacking in grey matter. And watch them wilt!

The solicitor's belittling and infuriating comment had been enough to cement her decision. It had left her without any room to manoeuvre. If he thought she was stupid to see Price Domenico, then Elizabeth Mary Alexandra Kent would prove him totally, irreconcilably, irrevocably, stupidly wrong!

After all, she was not guilty of negligent driving. She refused to accept the black mark against her faultless driving record. She was completely innocent. It was a travesty of justice that she be found in any wrong whatsoever. And how that police sergeant, who had seemed so nice and understanding, could have turned her statement into a charge of negligent driving was beyond her comprehension! It was dishonest. Deceitful. Indecent. She was going to fight that charge until proper justice was done.

The solicitor had pointed out that Price Domenico was a specialist in criminal law and did not take cases that were heard in the Court of Petty Sessions. He had said that she didn't have a hope of getting to see a barrister of his standing, let alone persuading him to defend her case. Elizabeth wished that petty-minded solicitor could see her now, sitting in this plush waiting-room, all primed for her appointment with Price Domenico.

She was not stupid. There were ways of going about things. And she was absolutely certain that

Price Domenico knew ways of going about things, too. After all, his father had been a leader of the Sydney underworld for decades. Only a few years ago the old man had been gunned down during a spate of gangland killings. The Domenicos of this world were capable of anything, and had proved it over and over again.

There were rumours at the Academy where Elizabeth worked that the son had taken over from the father. And that made sense. Price Domenico would see that he got his way, legally or illegally. It ran in the family. And explained why he never lost a case in court. It was even said that at the present moment he was very much involved in running illegal casinos.

Of course, nothing had ever been proved against him. If it had, he would have been disbarred. But he wasn't the first person to hide his illegal activities behind the façade of legality. And he wouldn't be the last.

But, in the circumstances that Elizabeth found herself in, it seemed to her that he was precisely the type of person she needed. Undoubtedly Price Domenico knew every loophole there was in the law, and surely he would be able to make mincemeat of the trumped-up charge against her?

It was just lucky that she had a ready entrée to him because of Ricky. Otherwise she might have had to wait months for an appointment. She was already learning that in this world it was more important whom you knew than what you knew.

As her gaze drifted around the waiting-room, she concluded that Price Domenico was not loath to demonstrate his success—which made her feel all the more secure about her decision. To have his offices in this prestigious building, with its views of Sydney Harbour, was certainly costing him a small fortune. He was not stinting on space or furnishings, either! The waiting-room alone was almost as big as her whole apartment, and much, much more luxurious. The beige carpet was at least an inch thick. Two brown leather chesterfields faced each other across a parquet-patterned coffee-table that looked in the antique class. The bronze sculpture that graced it was undoubtedly a collector's piece. Lush pot-plants broke up the arrangement of leather armchairs. The paintings on the walls were definitely originals. Price Domenico had money, and a lot of it.

All in all, Elizabeth decided that anyone who could pay for such a plush workplace had to be using ill-gotten gains. Or skirting around the taxation department. Which, in Price Domenico's case, made sense. If what she had heard at school was half-way true, there would be a lot of activities and dealings he would not want to declare to anyone, let alone the taxation department.

One certainty formed in Elizabeth's mind as she summed up the waiting-room: honesty didn't pay this much. Honesty didn't pay at all, she thought bleakly. Maybe it wasn't terribly ethical to seek the services of a man like Price Domenico, but, if it took legal skulduggery to beat legal skulduggery, why should she quibble? Her conscience was clear, and she had every right to have her name cleared.

If Price Domenico could do that for her, she was not about to question why he never lost his cases. She was not guilty. That was the important thing.

And no amount of well-meant advice was going to railroad her into letting any judge proclaim her anything but completely innocent!

The telephone on the antique oak desk buzzed and the blonde receptionist picked up the receiver. She was perfectly suited to this environment: elegant, good-looking, and with a figure that most men would find more aesthetic than any sculpture or paintings. Elizabeth watched her answer the call, wondering if she had more than a working relationship with her boss. Price Domenico was a widower, although he was only in his early thirties. And there were plenty of rumours about that! Elizabeth studied the blonde with hard-learnt cynicism. Was she employed because of her brains, or her willingness to satisfy the boss, no matter what demands he threw at her?

'Mr Domenico will see you now, Miss Kent.' The receptionist smiled, replacing the receiver and starting up from the desk to show the way.

Elizabeth glanced at her watch as she rose from the comfortable leather chesterfield. It was four forty-two. He had kept her waiting for only twelve minutes, which was undoubtedly very generous of him. Now that she had got this far, she hoped he would take the time to give her a proper hearing.

She was ushered into a room that would have been appropriate for the president of a worldwide company. The man working at the very large and magnificent mahogany desk did not look the part.

He was coatless, tieless, and the sleeves of his white shirt were rolled up as if he couldn't even stand the formal constriction of cuffs. Perhaps he thought the executive trappings of the room were statement enough. Or that he himself was above conventional dress. Elizabeth decided she was not impressed.

'Mr Domenico, here is Miss Kent,' the receptionist lilted, then quietly slipped out of the room as the barrister raised his head to acknowledge the introduction.

The splendours of his office became a blur. The moment their eyes met, the man at the desk commanded the focus of all Elizabeth's attention, and she found herself more impressed than she liked to feel. Perhaps it was the smile—faintly crooked, very white, and compelling in its whimsical charm. Or the eyes—a tigerish tawny-yellow that had a dangerous animal gleam about them. Or the long, lithe physique that unwound from his chair to stand over six feet tall. Or the tight mop of black curls that flopped on to his forehead.

Whatever it was, Elizabeth immediately felt on edge. It made her feel wary, defensive. She clutched her handbag with both hands in front of her—an instinctive but ineffective shield.

He came out from behind the desk and offered his hand. 'Miss Kent, how pleased I am to meet you! I can see now why my son is so enamoured of you. My own teachers were not nearly so attractive.'

His voice was deep and pleasant. It seemed to coil right down to her stomach. She took a deep breath to settle the flutter that had started there, then forced one hand off her bag. She touched his fingers briefly; the feeling was electric. She snatched her hand back in shock and clutched her handbag even more tightly. This was not what she had expected, and it did not encourage her in any shape or form. Her mind dictated that a man who looked and sounded this good just had to be bad.

Although she had deliberately mentioned her teacher-pupil relationship with his son when she had rung his receptionist for an appointment, that was totally irrelevant to the business in hand and she had to set him straight.

Her grey eyes automatically rejected the warmth in his greeting. 'You're very kind,' she said crisply, 'but I don't want you to be mistaken about me. I have not come about school business, Mr Domenico.'

The warmth died a quick death. There was a tightening about his face and body—relaxed grace turning to tensile steel. His mouth took on a thin, sardonic twist and a mocking light flicked into his eyes. 'Of course. From the reputation I enjoy at your school, it would only be extreme personal need that would bring you to me, Miss Kent,' he said with sweet acid. 'Please, take a seat.'

The subtle sting of his words left Elizabeth feeling uncomfortable. She never responded well to flattery, and she certainly hadn't expected Price Domenico to start the conversation by flattering her. She hadn't been prepared for it. His rebuke to her cold little reply fretted at her mind. Perhaps she should have complimented him on his son. All parents were indulgent where their children were concerned, and Ricky Domenico was the star of her class in more ways than one. She could say so with complete honesty.

But Price Domenico didn't give her the chance. He indicated a chair with a resigned wave of his hand, and turned his back on her. Elizabeth took the chair and waited until he had resumed his position behind the large desk. She looked up to find his tawny-yellow gaze making what appeared to be a derisive appraisal of her. Which made her feel even more uncomfortable, although she had no reason to doubt her choice of clothes.

Alpha Academy insisted that their teachers looked well-dressed and respectable in every way. Elizabeth complied as best she could within her budget. Today she had worn a mint-green linen suit with a white tailored blouse and white accessories. She wore all clothes well because she was taller than average and her figure was slim and neatly proportioned.

The rich mass of her dark brown hair was plaited into a thick coronet, the rather severe style emphasising the fine bone-structure of her face. Her grey eyes were large and darkly fringed, her nose straight and distinctly aristocratic, her mouth softly feminine, her ears small and delicately shaped. She was not a Botticelli painting, but there was that indefinable air of class about her that automatically drew attention.

Elizabeth was not aware—and she would have been outraged if she had known—that it was not her teaching ability or qualifications that had won her a position at Alpha Academy, but the manner in which she projected dignity and beauty. It was thought that she would be a good example for all the girls to follow.

The headmaster of this private and very exclusive school automatically selected his staff and students on the three Bs: Brains, Breeding and

Beauty. Elizabeth had topped the count on at least two of them. Ricky Domenico had topped the count on the other. If it had not been for his outstanding abilities he would never have been accepted as a pupil, although a hefty donation from his father had mollified the almost overwhelming objection to his breeding.

Alpha Academy had been founded as a school for specially gifted children. It was Elizabeth's responsibility to feed Ricky Domenico's remarkable brain, and others like it, but more importantly she projected the right air of high-class breeding—even if she was unaware of it herself.

Nor was she aware that it was precisely the same assumed breeding that now brought a cynical twist to Price Domenico's lips. He made her feel that she had just been scrutinised under a microscope. And she had come out of it feeling like a microbe, or a germ.

She forced herself to correct the first impression she had given him. 'It's a joy to teach your son, Mr Domenico. He is an exceptional child.'

She determinedly held his sardonic gaze and, after a short pause, he did respond, but not in a way that put Elizabeth any more at ease.

'I want the best education I can get for him, Miss Kent,' he drawled. 'Cost is no object. Although I sometimes wonder if the schools themselves understand their own philosophy. But that is a personal belief.' He smiled a grim, humourless smile. 'Now, how can I help you?'

A dark flush crept over her flawless olive skin. He certainly knew how to return a snub with interest. The pleasantries were definitely dispensed with.

Somehow this meeting was going wrong—not how Elizabeth had planned it at all. Price Domenico had upset everything. He was a very upsetting man. He was evoking reactions in her that she didn't like and didn't want. It was downright deceitful of him not to fit the image he ought to fit.

But she had to put that aside. She had come here for a purpose, and that purpose still had to be served. One way or another, she had to persuade Price Domenico to serve it for her. To the best of his ability.

In a concentrated attempt to regain control of the situation, Elizabeth tried to see his son in him. She could handle Ricky. Of course, Ricky was only five years old, but he did have black curly hair. And the jawline was similar. The eyes, unfortunately, were not the same colour at all. Ricky's were a friendly, guileless sherry-brown that automatically invited affectionate indulgence. But if she kept thinking about the look in those tawny-yellow eyes she wouldn't be able to speak at all. Elizabeth swallowed hard and came straight to the point.

'I've been charged with negligent driving,' she started boldly. 'And charged quite wrongly. I'm not guilty. Never was. And I don't want such a false and unfair conviction on my record. I would like you to fight it for me and prove my innocence.'

A hand moved across his face in apparent weariness. He looked at his watch. He sagged back in his chair and viewed her through narrowed eyes. 'I don't do that kind of work, Miss Kent,' he said flatly. 'It's really wasting my time.'

Elizabeth felt the blood draining from her face. Outright rejection. He hadn't even offered her the slimmest chance of an opening to pursue her argument. She hadn't realised, until this moment, how much she had been depending on a favourable result from this meeting. The sense of failure was so sharp, so devastating, that she was thrown completely off balance.

'So you're condemning me unheard—just like everyone else!' she burst out bitterly. The injustice of it all seemed to crystallise on the judgement she had most resented, and the words spilled from her lips before she could catch them back. 'My solicitor told me that I was stupid to come and see you. He said it was the most stupid thing he'd ever heard of...' The soul-scarred misery of other defeats made this one seem much worse. The bleakness of despair coated her voice as she added, 'I thought... you were my best chance... my only real hope...'

He frowned, impatiently it seemed, and Elizabeth bit her lip, mortified by the admissions she had made. To him, of all people! The quivery sense of having made a fool of herself was awful. She stood up, automatically stiffening her spine, squaring her shoulders, lifting her chin.

'I'm sorry for wasting your time,' she recited stiffly. 'I won't waste any more of it.' She swung quickly towards the door, painfully conscious of the need for a dignified withdrawal.

'Wait!'

The sharp ring of command made her hesitate in her step, and before she could recover her equilibrium Price Domenico was at her side, turning her around to face him again. His action brought them very close, his hands lightly grasping her upper arms. Startled, Elizabeth stared up at him in helpless confusion. He stared down at her, a conflict of interests warring across his face.

Something very alarming stirred inside Elizabeth. Her body trembled. Her mind was swamped with an awareness of his strong masculinity. Her eyes fastened on his lips, and she found herself wondering how they would feel on hers if he kissed her. Which was an appalling piece of insanity.

His broad chest rose and fell as he drew a quick breath. One of his hands dropped away and clenched into a fist at his side. The other slid down to her elbow.

'Come...sit down again. Perhaps I was too hasty. Since you came to consult me, you have a right to tell me your story. In your own way and in your own words. Then I will decide if I can be of some help to you.'

The words were some balm to her wounded pride, but the tone was brusque, and Elizabeth felt that they had been clipped out against his better judgement. However, he gave her little choice in the matter. He firmly steered her to the chair she had vacated, and saw her seated before turning back to his desk.

Elizabeth sat in a daze, still shaken by the swift and unwelcome sexual impact he had made on her. She hadn't even felt anything like that with the man she had married, nor with any of the men she had dated since being widowed. Not that there had been very many, and only on a very casual basis. Elizabeth had no intention of remarrying. She had even reverted to her maiden name. She didn't want any man having so much power over her life ever again.

Above all, not a man like Price Domenico!

CHAPTER TWO

ELIZABETH brought all her will-power to bear on getting herself under control. Price Domenico had given her another chance to interest him in her case. That was what she had to keep at the forefront of her mind. Everything else was to be forgotten. Promptly and effectively. He would get only disciplined reactions from her from now on.

He was frowning heavily as he drew some notepaper out of a drawer and set it on the desk-top in front of him. He picked up a gold pen, tapped it on the paper several times, then slowly beamed those disturbing eyes at her.

'Tell me the circumstances behind this charge of negligent driving, Miss Kent,' he invited briskly.

Elizabeth slowly explained what had happened. He was such a distracting person that she needed all the help Price Domenico could give her to bring out the facts. She kept noticing silly details about him as he noted things down: the long, supple fingers of his hands, the muscular strength of his bared forearms, the sensual curve of his lower lip, the rather Roman cast of his nose, the distinctive arch of his eyebrows, the way his hair curled neatly around his ears.

Slowly the picture of the accident emerged: the rain, the oil slick on the road, the boy on the bicycle who had skidded from the adjoining traffic-lane right in front of her car, the necessity to swerve to avoid hitting him, then crashing into the brick wall, being taken to the hospital still unconscious from concussion, the statement she had made to the policeman, and the subsequent charge.

'Apparently, if there were any eye-witnesses to the accident, they didn't wait around to give statements to the police. Neither did the boy on the bicycle. As far as the law is concerned, I skidded on the wet road and lost control of my vehicle. And they say I'm guilty of negligent driving when, in actual fact, I saved that boy's life,' she concluded bitterly.

He put his pen down. There was a sardonic twitch to his mouth as he raised his gaze to hers. 'In short, you have no corroboration for your story,' he commented drily.

Elizabeth stared him down with wintry eyes. 'I am not inventing this, Mr Domenico. I'm sure I told the policeman the same things, because it's the truth. But I was only just getting over the concussion when he questioned me, and maybe he paid more attention to some things than others. I don't understand why I've been charged, but I'm not lying to you.'

'I was not suggesting you were, Miss Kent. To most thinking people, the ways in which bureaucrats work are filled with mystery. To fight your case and win—there's the rub. The best way would be to find the witnesses. Any witness. The optimum would be to find the boy who rode the bicycle. And that would be a very costly business. Extremely so. If not impossible.'

He paused to let that sink in, then slowly added, 'In these circumstances, the most practical advice

I can give you is to pay the fine and forget the whole thing. You will have learnt something from the experience, even if it is dearly bought. In future, never make any statement to the police before consulting a solicitor. Particularly when you have concussion. You can save yourself a lot of trouble.'

His mouth curled into an ironic smile. 'Most people incriminate themselves. Even when they're innocent of any wrongdoing. They dig their graves with their mouths. When it comes to the law, silence *is* golden.'

Elizabeth's cheeks burned with angry colour. 'I am not guilty, Mr Domenico. I gave you a completely honest statement. I've given the same one to the police. They think I'm trying to exculpate myself. I see no reason why I should be penalised for something I didn't do. If there is any justice in this country——'

'Justice, Miss Kent, is an abstract ideal we like to dream about. In a pragmatic world, it counts for very little. The reality, more often than not, is a bad joke.' His voice was heavily coated with profound cynicism.

'Is that your way of saying you're not interested in fighting for me, Mr Domenico?' Elizabeth accused more than asked. 'Or for other people like me?'

'On the contrary,' he smoothly assured her, 'I'm simply warning you that, however innocent you are, you will still end up a victim of the law. If you fight this charge you will be a victim of costs. The inescapable fact is that you will be even more of a loser than you will be if you pay the fine. But...' He gave her a look that was chillingly similar to one of her father's—the kind that said it was time she got a well-earned lesson, and that his mind was bent on giving it to her. It made Elizabeth bristle with defiance. However, his next words were quiet and disarming. '...if it means so much to you, I'm willing to take your case on.'

The bristles retracted and Elizabeth's spirit lifted. 'How much money am I looking at?' She was determined not to be beaten on what she saw as a matter of personal honour.

He leaned forward, resting his elbows on the desk. There was a malicious gleam of satisfaction in his eyes as he ticked off the expenses, one by one, on his fingers.

'My fee in court is two hundred dollars an *hour*. We'll need a private investigator on the case to try to find some useful witnesses. His fee is four hundred dollars a day. No one can project at this stage how many days he will need. But if he has to canvas a very large area—several suburbs—in order to find the boy, your quest for justice will become exorbitantly expensive. Of course, if you're not overly concerned about many thousands of dollars, Miss Kent, and you don't care how much it costs to get your slate wiped clean...'

A cloud of bleak disillusionment settled over Elizabeth's mind. One of these days, perhaps she would learn the wisdom of not tilting at windmills. And yet... did the world have to be like this? Why did the cost of fighting for rightness always prove so dear? She could cope with the mental strain. She could even manage to rise above the emotional and physical wear and tear. But on this issue she was beaten on the financial front.

'Perhaps I could find the boy myself...' Her voice trailed away as the enormity of the task bore down on her—going from house to house, asking people about a month-old accident, and she would only be able to do it at weekends. Besides which, there was that history assignment to be researched and written—which was so important if she was to pass her course—and the...

'More than you expected, Miss Kent?' came an insidiously mocking voice.

Elizabeth had been so beset by the money problem that she had forgotten that hint of malice in Price Domenico's eyes as he had begun his exposition on costs. She glanced up sharply, niggled by this new, unpleasant tone from him. Had he been playing some obscure cat-and-mouse game with her—pretending to be interested and concerned because of her connection with his son, all the while anticipating the cut-off punchline?

'By your reckoning, I can't afford it, Mr Domenico,' she said flatly. 'I can't even afford you.'

He shrugged and leaned back in his chair again, uncaring of her plight. He had made his important point—forced her to face the kind of reality she had probably never once had to face in all of her cosy high-bred life. It had been a totally irrational impulse to stop her from leaving earlier, yet there was something about her...

He angrily suppressed the feeling, a taunting challenge in his eyes as he quietly but very deliberately put forward another suggestion. 'A young lady of your class must have considerable financial assets in the background, Miss Kent. Surely your family would be interested in helping, if it means so much to you?'

Elizabeth burned with indignation. He was definitely mocking her. Just because she couldn't afford him. And he was probably rolling in millions from playing the law any way he liked!

'I have no family, Mr Domenico,' she bit out angrily. 'The only income I have is what I earn. I'm sorry to disappoint your expectations of me, but I am just an ordinary person. What little I have was got from hard—honest—work. Which is something some people might not know all that much about.'

She had surprised him. No doubt about that. But it gave Elizabeth no satisfaction. It infuriated her that she should be so unable to defend her rights. The rich could pay for justice. People like Price Domenico could wriggle their way around it. But she was a victim with no avenue for redress.

She hated him in that moment. Hated the whole system that had brought her to this intolerable impasse. But she hated him most of all, because he had played her along, thinking she was stupid, reeling her in for the kill. And he was so smug in his smartness!

Elizabeth didn't stop to think. A turbulent combination of pride, fury and frustration drove her beyond the tenets by which she had always led her life.

'If that's all you can say...' she seethed, and lifted her head in aristocratic determination not to be put down '...if that's the only conclusion you can come to, then I must ask you the cost—the final cost of doing it another way.'

He shook his head in apparent bewilderment. 'What other way?'

Her grey eyes stabbed at Price Domenico with belligerent purpose. 'I want you to fix it. The law.'

He laughed. 'I regret that fixing laws is not within my power, Miss Kent.'

'Let's not play games, Mr Domenico,' she flashed back at him, fiercely resenting his amusement. And evasion. 'People like you are fixing things all the time. That's how this rotten world works, isn't it? That's why you're so wealthy. But just for once you can do some fixing in order to right a wrong. So, to get back to the critical point in question—how much will it cost?'

His face tightened and all expression blanked from his eyes. 'I don't think I understand you, Miss Kent,' he said in a low, dangerous monotone.

Elizabeth was not in the mood to heed danger signals. She plunged on with reckless determination. 'I don't know how to phrase these things. We all know it's done. You've got the connections to have this charge dropped, or quashed, or whatever the term is. I want to know how much that costs in the pragmatic world you live in, Mr Domenico. Where justice is a joke! I'm sure you understand.'

He sat there as if carved in stone. He didn't so much as flicker an eyelid. 'Why are you so sure, Miss Kent?' he asked very quietly.

She eyed him derisively. 'You might put up a respectable façade, Mr Domenico, but underneath it all you wangle things your way by whatever means you've set up for your purpose. Favours swapped for favours under the table. Isn't that how it goes? I mean, with your father... being what he was...'

Suddenly, she couldn't go on. Hearing her own words—it was so distasteful, alien to everything she had ever lived by. Shock at her own madness paralysed her mind.

A cold, bleak look settled on Price Domenico's face. He sagged back in his chair, his whole body expressing weary defeat. His mouth twisted into a savage little grimace. Then he looked up at her and the mockery was back in his eyes.

'Tell me, Miss Kent. How much can you afford... for your brand of justice?'

Shock piled on top of shock. He was accepting... and a perverse kind of pride wouldn't let her retreat. 'A thousand dollars,' she replied defiantly. She would show him that she would pay whatever was necessary to clear her name.

Then she remembered the costs he had quoted to her before. In his world a thousand dollars was almost nothing. He probably charged that much to make a telephone call. And, with a growing sense of unease, her mind started to encompass all she was asking. Elizabeth lifted hesitant, uncertain eyes.

'Perhaps... two thousand? I think... if I have to... I could get two thousand dollars.'

He seemed to stare straight through her, as if she wasn't there. Elizabeth was filled with panicky doubts. She was off her brain to have asked him in the first place. And then to have persisted!

Two thousand was her absolute limit. She didn't know anything about this kind of thing. She didn't really want to know. But it was also grossly unfair that she should be victimised by the law when it was supposed to protect innocent, well-meaning people like her.

There was nothing more that she could say. She watched Price Domenico with almost frenzied apprehension. He remained silent for a dreadfully long time. He nodded his head slowly, at irregular intervals, as if mentally ticking off points. Finally he appeared to come to some decision.

'I'll do it for you,' he said tersely. 'I'll take your case. I'll see what can be done.'

Relief surged through her, only to be followed by a wave of confusion. Did he mean he was going to take her case legitimately—or the other way? How could she tell? He would think her even more stupid if she asked. Lord! What had she got herself into?

Price Domenico could be fobbing her off—or even promising her what he was not going to deliver. She couldn't afford to believe him, nor could she trust him. The mere fact that he was taking her case showed that he couldn't be trusted with money—would do anything for it. Her brush with the law was enough to convince Elizabeth that she couldn't trust anyone. And it was well known that there was no honesty among thieves.

'You . . . haven't named your price.'

He waved a dismissive hand. 'A thousand dollars will be fine.'

There was definitely something wrong here. The tone of his reply was uninterested, almost contemptuous. It seemed incredible that he was doing it so cheaply. She tried to penetrate his thoughts.

Tawny-golden eyes suddenly locked on to hers—hard and burning with malevolence. 'It's usual in these arrangements... for the money to be placed up-front. It's taken as a gesture of... shall we say... goodwill?'

'I don't trust you, Mr Domenico,' she retorted fiercely. 'And I'm not that gullible.' He was bad, all right. Bad all through. But he was not going to get the better of her. 'I'll give you two hundred dollars now. The other eight hundred dollars you will get when I'm found not guilty. Or the case is dismissed.'

'As you wish,' he said coldly.

Elizabeth wasn't sure how to take that. But she had stated her terms, so she had no other course left than to deliver on them. She withdrew her cheque-book from her handbag and started to write out a cheque for the two hundred dollars.

'Please...'

The sarcastic drawl jerked her head up.

'... in the circumstances... only cash.'

A hot tide of mortification flooded her face, right to the roots of her hair. 'I'm sorry... I... I didn't think.'

He shook his head, his face contorting with frustration—or was it revulsion? 'Pay me when the case is finished. If I win it. And in cash,' he rapped out tersely, then thrust himself out of his chair and stalked over to the window which looked out over the old convict prison of Fort Denison in Sydney Harbour.

He stood there, apparently taking in the view, his back turned to her in a rejection so complete that Elizabeth felt totally confused. She stood up, yet somehow she couldn't quite bring herself to walk out—not without determining something more conclusive than this unspoken dismissal.

'You'll inform me when . . .'

'Certainly.'

Still she dithered, her heart hammering painfully in her chest. She wanted him to turn around. Wanted . . . she didn't know what she wanted, but every instinct was screaming for some better resolution.

'Thank you, Mr Domenico,' she said huskily from a throat that had gone bone-dry.

He said nothing. He remained obdurately motionless.

'Good day to you,' she added with stiff formality.

He turned slowly, and looked back at her with cold, remote eyes. 'It is not a good day, Miss Kent. But one I'm quite familiar with, nevertheless,' he said with quiet savagery. 'I'll see you next in court.'

'In court?' Elizabeth echoed weakly. Her conscience was insisting that two wrongs didn't make a right. But she didn't even know if they were talking about two wrongs any more. This conversation had gone right off the rails.

He gave her a grim smile. 'I always take my cases to court, Miss Kent. Unless the opposition wants to settle them first. I am . . . a *barrister*.' The deliberate emphasis he gave the word confused her even further.

'I see,' she murmured, though she wasn't at all sure that she did see.

It was almost as if steel shutters closed over his face, barring her from any part of his life. 'That is all now. Good day, Miss Kent. And goodbye.'

Two very painful spots burnt into her cheeks. 'I'll . . . I'll bring the cash with me . . . to the court, I mean.'

'You do that, Miss Kent.'

For a few very jittery moments Elizabeth thought she had been mistaken about him—that he wasn't a criminal at all—but his last seething words had dispelled the ridiculous doubt. The threatening power of the man choked the breath in her throat. His eyes held hers in a kind of magnetic thrall for several seconds. It took all her will-power to wrench herself away from him and walk to the door.

She did not look back as she left, but the hairs on the back of her neck prickled until his door was well and truly shut behind her. Every nerve in her body was shrieking that Price Domenico was a very dangerous man, and her mind throbbed with the knowledge that she had just done a very dangerous thing.

As Elizabeth emerged into the ordinary city scurry on Bridge Street, she felt crushed by the thought that she had been truly stupid—more so than she had ever been in her whole life. But it was already too late to retract what she had said and done. Just the idea of facing Price Domenico again turned her bones to water.

There was nothing—nothing at all that she could do about it now.

CHAPTER THREE

ELIZABETH had no recollection of the train-trip from the inner city out to Chatswood, nor of the ten-minute walk to the apartment-block where she lived. She was putting the key into her front-door lock before she had even realised she was home.

As she stepped into her living-room and shut the rest of the world out, her gaze swept around her modest possessions with bleak irony. If Price Domenico had assumed that her Chatswood address meant that she came from a moneyed family, he could not have been more wrong. There were a good many parts of Chatswood that housed wealthy people, but this apartment-block was old and had no pretensions to being fashionable.

The Axminster carpet was very serviceable and an uninteresting grey. Elizabeth's furniture had been acquired, piece by piece, from second-hand shops. She had covered the cushions of the armchairs and sofa with a pretty floral fabric in lemon, blue and white, and it helped to brighten the room. The only expensive items she owned were the television and video sets, neither of which she had purchased until she had saved up the full price for them.

She remembered all too well the shock of being dispossessed of everything after her husband's death. Simon had never been content to wait for anything. All smart people work on an overdraft, he had jeered whenever she expressed doubts about his financial juggling. Elizabeth was determined never to be in debt to anyone, for anything, ever again.

Which was another thing that worried her about the business with Price Domenico. He had said she need only pay him the thousand dollars if he won the case. How could that possibly be right?

She wandered into the kitchenette to take some tablets for her headache. It didn't matter how she tried to justify what she had done, it still came out wrong. If only she had had more money.

She could have saved on the rent over the years if she had sublet the second bedroom in her apartment. But it was so small, and she had not wanted to share her living quarters with anyone else. Besides, she needed quiet solitude in order to study, and a place to keep all her books and papers.

If she had fully insured her little second-hand car, instead of only taking out third-party insurance, the accident would not have been such a total write-off. She would have had money in hand. But the extra expense hadn't seemed worth it at the time. She was such a careful driver. In the ten years she had carried a driving licence, she had never incurred the tiniest bump or scratch, let alone crashed a car.

She had accepted that disaster as one of life's extremely frustrating tribulations. It had undoubtedly contributed to her sense of injustice over the charge of negligent driving. Until this afternoon, Elizabeth had been satisfied that she was managing her life very well. Now she was in a mess, and she had no one to blame except herself. She wished she had never heard of Price Domenico, let alone gone to see him.

But wishful thinking wasn't going to change anything. It was too late now—what was done was done. The most practical course to take was to wait the whole thing out, pay over the money, and put it all behind her as quickly as she could.

The whole matter preyed on her mind so much that Elizabeth couldn't concentrate long enough to do any effective study that night. She didn't sleep very well, either. She took herself off to Alpha Academy the next morning in a dismal frame of mind.

The school was situated at Wahroonga, one of the higher-class suburbs on the North Shore train-line, and it was no real hardship for Elizabeth to catch a train instead of driving to work. She often ran into some of the older pupils on the train, or walking up to the school-grounds, but this morning she did not invite anyone's company. She gave the barest of greetings to the few staff members she met as she signed in for the day, then secluded herself in her classroom as soon as she could.

Which turned out to be a mistake.

Mrs Wetherington-Jones tracked her down and buttonholed her for the whole half-hour before class began, regaling her with details and cautions about dear little Stephanie's health. Mrs Wetherington-Jones had three *brilliant* grandchildren at Alpha Academy. Elizabeth had the honour of teaching the youngest.

Dear little Stephanie's avant-garde drawings and paintings were a clear indication of great artistic talent, according to her grandmother. Unfortunately, the spoiled little girl had an artistic temperament to match, as well as a precocious leaning towards hypochondria. She tried Elizabeth's patience to the limit. So did Mrs Wetherington-Jones.

Particularly when she started on Ricky Domenico.

'It's not for me to interfere with what you do in the classroom, Miss Kent,' she began, with every obvious intention of interfering, 'but Stephanie seems to have developed a most unsuitable crush on that Domenico boy. Apparently she was seated next to him during the reading lesson yesterday. I would be obliged if you seated her next to someone else in future.'

She fixed her haughty blue eyes meaningfully on Elizabeth and waited expectantly for her assent. She was a tall, handsome woman, somewhere in her fifties, and very much imbued with her own sense of self-importance. She had been born into a line of blue-blooded Liberal politicians, the family wealth having accrued over generations of power, and she was a do-gooder of the worst kind. *Good* meant meeting her personal standards of need and want.

Expedience was clearly the order of the day, but for some reason Elizabeth bridled against Mrs Wetherington-Jones's prejudice. It reminded her of Price Domenico's cynicism yesterday. He had judged her as being cut from the same mould as this woman.

'Ricky is a nice boy, Mrs Wetherington-Jones,' she said gently. 'Most of the girls in my class have a crush on him. Stephanie will be very put out if I make a point of separating her from him. They are very young, you know,' she added in soft appeasement.

Mrs Wetherington-Jones did not bend. From the top of her stylishly coiffured head to the handmade fashion shoes on her narrow aristocratic feet she stiffened with displeasure. 'It is never too soon to discourage undesirable relationships, Miss Kent.' The prudish mouth tightened. 'I am in complete sympathy with the headmaster's high ideals in education, but there are limits to be observed where society is concerned. Good looks do not make up for bad breeding. Nor does intellect. I'm sure you understand me, Miss Kent.'

Her last words carried an uncomfortable echo of Elizabeth's own words to Price Domenico. Elizabeth felt sickened by them. 'I'll do what I can, Mrs Wetherington-Jones,' she said weakly, telling herself that Ricky was better off to be spared Stephanie's company, anyway.

Elizabeth was relieved when the school-bell rang and she had the excuse of school assembly to escape from Mrs Wetherington-Jones's presence.

But her morning classes were not easy. Ricky Domenico kept distracting her. Not because of any misbehaviour. On the contrary, he was as amenable as usual, almost diffident in his natural ability to outshine everyone else in her class. But she kept looking for the father in the son, and feeling more and more confused about Price Domenico.

'Daddy said he met you yesterday,' Ricky confided to her when she checked his spelling, which was perfectly accurate no matter what words she gave him. The boy had once told her he had been reading newspapers on his father's knee for as long as he could remember. His sherry-brown eyes glowed up at her in pleasurable expectation.

'Yes,' she murmured in reply, an embarrassed flush warming her cheeks. 'I went to see him about some business.'

Ricky was not interested in business, for which Elizabeth was grateful. She had been caught off guard by his comment. She had not anticipated that Price Domenico would have mentioned her visit to his son.

Ricky gave her a shy little smile. 'Daddy thought you were beautiful, too.'

Elizabeth's flush grew painful and her heart gave a peculiar lurch. Had Price Domenico felt the same sense of physical attraction that had knocked her off balance? Was that why he had called her back after his initial rejection of her case? But then he had been so unsympathetic . . . mocking . . . and contemptuous. If he had thought her beautiful, he certainly didn't want to feel attracted to her, any more than she liked feeling attracted to him.

'How nice of you to say so, Ricky!' she muttered tightly, then set the boy some more work to effectively squash any other disturbing comments.

The man was almost certainly indulging his son, keeping what he really thought about her to himself. But she was glad that he had said nothing to undermine the unquestioning trust Ricky had in her as a teacher. Shame wormed around Elizabeth's sense of guilt. To have asked Price Domenico's help in the way she had made her just as much a criminal as he was.

What madness had possessed her?

And what if he wasn't a criminal?

At the morning tea-break, Elizabeth was waylaid on her way to the staff-room by the headmaster's secretary. 'Miss Kent, Mr Fairchild would like you to join him in his office.'

The invitation was of course a command, but it was nothing unusual. The morning-tea chat with a teacher was part of the headmaster's policy of keeping his finger on the pulse of the school. Elizabeth wished Mr Fairchild had picked some other morning for her pep talk, but she masked her inner agitation with a cool air of confidence, thanked the secretary, and complied with the command without question.

The administrative centre of the school was in fact a beautiful old mansion. The headmaster's office was situated off the entrance foyer and was a magnificent high-ceilinged room, its walls beautifully panelled in cedar. Leather-bound books filled glass-fronted bookcases; proudly framed photographs of celebrated students demonstrated the prowess of Alpha Academy—their names printed in gold leaf on a board of honour; the headmaster's academic degrees were also framed and prominently displayed, but Mr Fairchild himself was the natural focal point of the room.

Behind his huge cedar desk he ruled the school from a chair which had the dimensions of a throne, centred perfectly in front of the tall bay window. He was the arch-image of an authoritarian figure: over six feet tall, big but not fat, his face strong-boned and handsome in a rugged masculine sense, his eyes a piercing blue, his thick dark hair impressively sprinkled with grey.

He rose with towering charm as Elizabeth entered the room, smiling indulgently at her, complimenting her on her appearance, inviting her to take the chair opposite him, even pouring her a cup of tea from the exquisite china tea-service which was set on a silver tray on his desk.

Elizabeth took it all with the proverbial pinch of salt. While she had been almost awed by the man and his idealistic drive for excellence when he had first interviewed her for the vacant position on his staff, after two months at the school Elizabeth was well aware of the other factors operating behind the façade of the great educator.

He settled back on his chair and smoothly cut to the point of his invitation. 'A pity young Stephanie Wetherington-Jones is in the same class as the Domenico boy.' He gave a much-put-upon sigh, then raised his eyebrows in questioning concern. 'You settled that problem this morning?'

Elizabeth sipped her tea, hoping to calm the squeamish flutter in her stomach before answering. 'I assured Mrs Wetherington-Jones I would do what I could to keep the two children separated, Mr Fairchild. But Stephanie is very self-willed. And to be frank with you, Ricky Domenico outshines every other boy in the class in looks and ability. There is a limit to what can be controlled in a classroom. Without being tyrannical, it is impossible to stop them playing together at recess——'

'Yes, yes, I see your point.' His frown was full of vexation. 'Difficult situation. Impossible to deny the boy. He promises to be as outstanding as his father. Totally impossible in the face of what Alpha Academy stands for.'

Elizabeth had been in so much mental and emotional turmoil over Price Domenico that the headmaster's reference to him sparked a curiosity that made short shrift of her usual sense of cautious discretion. 'Was Ricky's father an outstanding student?'

Her question earned a grimace of frustration. 'Price Domenico was always *dux* of his class at Fort Street Boys' High School. And graduated with the highest honours in law from Sydney University. You don't get any higher than that, Miss Kent.'

Fort Street! It was the most prestigious public high school in the whole state. Its pupils were the intellectual élite, and even the bottom student of any class there would be recognised as a top student anywhere else. And Price Domenico had led all the rest!

Then to be scholastically in a class by himself when he graduated in law—no one else able to match his brilliance—no wonder the solicitor had been so scornful about her going to see him about a negligent driving charge!

But Price Domenico had seen her. And accepted the case. Under the most dubious circumstances. If he was so brilliantly smart, why had he done that?

'All the more remarkable, considering the nature of his background,' the headmaster added with a curl of distaste.

Elizabeth couldn't stand the treadmill of her thoughts another minute. She was desperate to know the truth. 'I was wondering about that, Mr Fairchild,' she said tentatively. 'I've heard rumours...'

She received a beetling frown of disapproval that would have made most people quail. But Elizabeth's father had left her immune to such tactics. She stared back, determined on an answer.

'We do not deal in gossip at Alpha Academy, Miss Kent,' came the frosty reproof.

Elizabeth stubbornly ignored it. 'Mr Fairchild, it is my responsibility to deal with a situation which smacks of discrimination. The boy is not guilty of anything except being born into his family. Over which he had no choice or control,' she reminded him. 'I appreciate the contribution made to this school by the Wetherington-Jones family, but I would feel much better about what I'm being asked to do if you have some cogent reason——'

'Miss Kent!' he snapped, cutting her off in mid-sentence. The piercing blue eyes stabbed her into silence. 'The good of Alpha Academy comes first and foremost. Let that be clearly understood. No child comes ahead of that.'

He waited pointedly for Elizabeth's submission to this principle. It was not a principle Elizabeth cared for at this particular moment. The system against the rights of the individual! It was precisely that kind of victimisation that she had been fighting yesterday.

And look where that landed you, her mind mocked. Do you want to lose your job on top of everything else?

Reluctantly, and with considerable difficulty, Elizabeth quelled the rebellion in her heart and gave the expected answer. The common-sense answer. But she hated every word of it.

'Of course the good of the school comes first, Mr Fairchild.' Then, with unrelenting persistence, she added, 'But I shall be able to make better judgements if I am better informed. If Ricky's father is . . . shall we say—a dangerous person . . .'

The headmaster frowned. 'You must handle this situation tactfully. The boy mustn't realise that any discrimination is taking place. Mr Domenico is not a person to be crossed. Neither is Mrs Wetherington-Jones. Let us try to keep the peace between them. If it came to a stand-up fight, I think Mr Domenico would tear her to shreds. He is that dangerous.'

Elizabeth's heart sank. 'You know that for a fact, sir?'

The question earned an angry glare. 'You can take my word for it, Miss Kent. Whatever else Price Domenico is, or isn't, he is a man who wields power with ruthless disregard for any finer principles. Even if he knows they exist. I would think he was totally amoral.' He put on his lofty face. 'However, our job is to steer fine intellects to higher purposes. Richard Domenico is a challenge, Miss Kent. I have every confidence that you will steer the right course for him and for the school.'

It was a dismissal.

Elizabeth stood up. 'Thank you for your confidence, sir.' She gave him a cool little smile.

Mr Fairchild returned a pontifical nod.

Elizabeth departed, convinced that she had not been wrong about Price Domenico after all. Clearly he had brought some pressure to bear on the headmaster to accept Ricky at the school. The kind of pressure she had assumed he could apply to get the charge of negligent driving dropped...or whatever.

Dangerous . . . and totally amoral.

The words haunted Elizabeth for days—weeks. But as the weeks turned into months, she managed to drive the business with Price Domenico to the back of her mind—some of the time—when she wasn't face to face with his son.

The first school-term ended at Easter. During the vacation she travelled up to Armidale to attend the residential school for external students at the University of New England. She enjoyed every minute of her five days there. Although she had lectures from virtually nine to five, the mental exhaustion from listening and frantically taking notes was quickly dispelled by the exhilarating evenings.

There was always a party to go to. Elizabeth loved mixing with the other students who, like her, were getting their university degrees the hard way. They exchanged ideas, swapped stories about their lonely struggles to achieve, and generally had a supercharged time away from the normal routine of their lives.

She could even have started a romance if she had wanted to. She enjoyed the marked attentions of two attractive, intelligent men who obviously admired her mind as well as her femininity. Not once did either of them imply that she was stupid in any way. On the contrary, they accorded her ideas and opinions every respect. But neither man made any real impact on her—not the kind of impact that Price Domenico had.

Which was such a discomfiting thought that Elizabeth did her utmost to bury it under a pile of feverish ambitions. She came home fired up not only to pass her chosen subjects, but to get credits in them, or even distinctions. And next year maybe she would do an honours course. Or start a law degree, so she would never get caught out in a legal bungle ever again.

The second school-term began. Stephanie Wetherington-Jones, in a fit of pique, started calling Ricky Domenico the teacher's pet. This made Elizabeth's job a bit tricky for a while, because Ricky was delighted by the epithet and not at all offended. He would have hung around Elizabeth all day if she had let him, but she had to be very firm about giving every pupil an equal amount of attention. Even Stephanie.

A political sex-scandal blew up in the newspapers. A Member of Parliament was forced to resign over his apparent involvement in brothels and drug-dealing. The conversation in the school staff-room was dominated by whether he was guilty or not, and whether he would be brought to trial, and what repercussions there would be from the whole affair. Elizabeth took no part in the conversations. They reminded her too forcefully of Price Domenico's background and the scandal over his wife's death.

And then, when she had almost begun to believe that the charge of negligent driving had somehow got mislaid in the police files, or been dropped altogether, the letter came from Price Domenico.

It was totally impersonal, stating the date and time set for the hearing and the number of the courtroom where it would be held.

There was only one good thing about it. The date was during the mid-year school break, so Elizabeth did not have to ask the headmaster for a day off.

She stared at the bold, black-inked signature at the bottom of the letter for a long time, her pulse beating erratically, her nerves slowly deteriorating into a jangling mess.

Price Domenico...

There was no escaping the inevitable fact that she now had to face him again. And she was not at all sure that the issues between them were clear-cut. She was not even sure what the issues were—but in the recesses of her mind she determined that, whatever Price Domenico did, she would retain her dignity and not let him confuse her with the kind of feelings he had evoked last time. That had to be wrong!

CHAPTER FOUR

THE day of the court hearing arrived. It was a bleak morning—cold and grey and promising rain. Elizabeth dithered over whether to take an umbrella or not. It would mean changing her handbag for a bigger one which could carry the cumbersome article. And then she would have to select other clothes as well, since her bigger handbag was black and would look out of place with her brown suit.

In the end she decided she couldn't risk getting wet on the walk to Chatswood Station. The thought of facing Price Domenico in a damp and bedraggled state was enough to force her back to the wardrobe, and although she had previously discounted the deep violet suit as a little too extrovert for a court appearance, a burst of belligerent female vanity reversed the decision.

After all, why shouldn't she look her best? Her clothes weren't going to sway the judgment on her case. The truth was the truth—and she was innocent! Besides, she suspected that her brown suit might bring a glint of cynical mockery to Price Domenico's tawny-yellow eyes. She didn't need that on top of everything else!

She dressed in a mood of defiance and even applied a more vibrant make-up than usual, highlighting her cheekbones with a subtle blusher and emphasising her eyes with a dark grey liner and a hint of violet shadow. She fiddled with her hair for a long time, playing with various styles before resigning herself to the safest course of plaiting it into the usual coronet. At least it stayed tidy that way—rain, hail or shine—and she certainly didn't want Price Domenico to think she was trying to attract his eye.

Because she wasn't!

He was not the type of man she would ever want to attract.

Her hands shook a little as they transferred the thousand dollars from the brown handbag to the black. She had never carried so much money in cash before. It made her nervous. She was half tempted to tear the envelope open to count the ten hundred-dollar bills again, but she knew that was absurd. She had checked the amount twice before sealing the envelope.

It did not rain on her walk to the railway station, but it poured down in sheets the moment she boarded the train. However, by the time Elizabeth emerged from Town Hall Station, the sharp shower had blown over and a weak sunshine was breaking through the clouds. She decided this was a good omen. Luck was on her side today. And she needed every bit of it to get her through the ordeal ahead of her.

She had no idea how Price Domenico meant to go about winning her case, and she didn't want to think about it. She just wanted it over and done with. Behind her.

Her apprehension that something might delay her on the way to the court-house did not eventuate, and she arrived an hour early. Rather than pace the floor and get herself into a nervous stew over what might or might not happen, Elizabeth sat in on the court hearing ahead of hers.

It was another accident case, with two sets of people disputing which driver had been in the wrong. Their evidence was diametrically opposed to each other's. Elizabeth couldn't tell who was lying, but somebody had to be. The barristers from both sides hammered away at the witnesses, and Elizabeth found her mouth getting drier and drier at the thought of being put through the same kind of questioning. She slipped out of the courtroom to get a drink of water.

'Excuse me, Miss...'

Elizabeth turned to see the man rising from the bench on the opposite side of the corridor. A woman and boy remained seated. All of them were looking hopefully at her.

'Could you tell us if the case in there is almost over?' He nodded to the woman. 'The wife here has an urgent desire to go...but it's almost time for our case and we're not sure...'

'Your case?' Elizabeth frowned. 'But my case is next. I asked the court-clerk and he——'

'You're Miss Kent?' the man cut in.

'Yes,' Elizabeth answered, wondering how this stranger knew her name.

His eyes beamed approval at her as he thrust out his hand. 'Well, we're mighty pleased to meet you, and we're terribly sorry you've been put in this fix, Miss Kent. I'm Harry Sefton. This is my wife, Heather, and my son, Mark. Your quick reaction in not hitting our boy with your car saved Mark's life. And we've come to set the record straight.'

Elizabeth dazedly shook hands with all three of them. 'You were the one on the bike?' she asked. The boy looked to be about eleven or twelve. It seemed incredible that Price Domenico had found him.

Or had he?

A ghastly suspicion slithered through Elizabeth's mind as she stared at the oh, so convenient witness who would undoubtedly win her case for her. And add to the long line of courtroom successes by Price Domenico.

'Yes, miss. I didn't know what to do when you crashed, so I rushed home to get help,' the boy explained sheepishly.

'He was in such a state,' Heather Sefton put in quickly. 'Shivering and babbling so incoherently, it took us a while to understand what had happened. Then, when Harry got to the scene of the accident, the ambulance was just pulling away.'

'I went to the hospital and hung around until they said you were all right,' Harry added, anxious to show his concern. 'They were terribly busy that night. Didn't want me bothering them. There were a lot of accident cases coming in. Caused by the rain, I expect. I sure am sorry about what happened to you, Miss Kent.'

'We should have left a note for you,' his wife said apologetically, 'but we're glad to have the chance to thank you now.' She hugged the boy close to her. 'Mark is very precious to us.'

They all sounded so genuine. They looked genuine. Elizabeth desperately wanted to believe them. But if it was some kind of scam she was getting for her thousand dollars...

'Here comes Mr Domenico!' the boy cried excitedly, and wriggled out of his mother's embrace.

They turned to watch the man of the moment stride down the corridor towards them. Elizabeth felt punch-drunk with doubts and fears, and the appearance of Price Domenico on the scene did nothing to ease her inner agitation.

The barrister's wig eliminated the softening effect his black curly hair might have had, and seemed to highlight the ruthless strength of his features, giving him a predatory look that his tigerish eyes did nothing to eliminate as they fastened on Elizabeth. Her stomach felt as if it were turning inside out as he advanced on her, his black gown billowing around him with each stalking step. He looked almost satanic—infinitely dangerous—the garb of the law a mockery of the man he was underneath: a man who would recognise no law but his own.

Having stripped Elizabeth of any coherent thought with the formidable power of his presence, he turned his gaze to the Seftons, his face visibly softening as they greeted him warmly.

'I see you've all met,' he remarked, flicking a bare acknowledgement at Elizabeth as he shook hands with all three of the Seftons. He didn't offer his hand to Elizabeth.

She was seized by a dreadful panic. Stupid or not, she had to know the truth before she walked into that courtroom. She had to know beyond all reasonable doubt. 'Mr Domenico, may I have a word with you in private?' she said forcefully, cutting through the friendly chat with the witnesses.

He gave her a look that would have shrivelled a less hardy person, but it served only to stiffen

Elizabeth's spine. Before either he or she could say another word, the Seftons retired, leaving them alone together.

'Well, Miss Kent?' The tawny-yellow eyes snapped with impatience.

She flushed, her heart beating overtime. 'I have to know if those people are real.'

One eyebrow arched sardonically. 'Do you suffer from hallucinations, Miss Kent?'

'Don't be ridiculous!' she snapped, too churned up to keep her language polite. 'You know perfectly well what I mean. Is that truly the boy or did you fix this?'

His face tightened. Something dangerous glittered in his eyes. 'Do you care, Miss Kent?' he asked acidly.

'Of course I care!' she said with feverish passion. 'I don't want anyone perjuring themselves on my behalf. Justice might be a bad joke, but telling lies under oath . . . is . . . is . . .'

'I understood that all you cared about was clearing your name . . . one way or another,' he taunted.

'I didn't mean . . .' She floundered hopelessly in the face of her own words, then finally dredged her gaze up to his in agonised appeal. 'I can't go through with this unless those people are genuine.'

His mouth twisted in malicious mockery. 'Well, well! A little qualm of conscience wriggling through your blue blood, Miss Kent?' Then suddenly his eyes were blazing at her in unadulterated contempt. 'Do you seriously imagine that I would ever lay myself open to a charge of fixing witnesses? That I would hand to you the power to get me disbarred?' His voice gathered a venomous hostility. 'I didn't get where I am by being a fool, Miss Kent. And I'm not entirely stupid.'

The doors to the courtroom opened and people came streaming out.

'Our turn, Miss Kent,' Price Domenico said with a silky change of tone. He smiled, but the smile didn't get anywhere near his eyes. 'And may I compliment you on your choice of clothes. I prefer to see all flags flying than a servile display of cringing hypocrisy. And when you go on the stand, please remember to tell the truth . . . exactly. That's all I want from you.'

He turned towards the door. Elizabeth stood stock-still, stunned by the violence of feeling behind Price Domenico's verbal attack on her. He turned back and took her arm in a punishing grip. His eyes stabbed through her shock, brutally commanding her attention.

'One more thing—keep your cool. Don't say anything you don't know. Having got your day in court, Miss Kent, I trust you will not do or say anything stupid.'

'I'm not stupid!' she cried, reacting heatedly to the goad that had dogged her life.

His eyes flicked a contemptuous dismissal of her protest. He steered her towards the door. The heat and strength of his grasp piled confusion on top of confusion. Elizabeth felt caught by the man and the situation, and she had absolutely no control over either. He escorted her into the courtroom and seated her at the front. Next to him.

The magistrate looked down at them from his elevated bench, an amused curiosity lifting the sternness from his face. 'We are not accustomed to seeing you here, Mr Domenico,' he remarked quizzically. 'Are we about to be treated to some esoteric point of law that I should be warned about?'

'I doubt that this case will test Your Honour in any way whatsoever,' was the dry response. 'Nothing could be more elementary.'

The magistrate looked unconvinced. 'Let's hope it's worth your time, Mr Domenico?' he commented, a question still hanging in his voice.

'Very much so, Your Honour,' Price Domenico drawled. 'It is a matter of personal honour.'

'Ah!'

Elizabeth burned with embarrassment as the magistrate's stare shifted to her. He examined her minutely with speculative interest. Then he gave a self-satisfied little smile which suggested that her appearance beside Price Domenico explained everything.

Which confused Elizabeth even further. She knew that Price Domenico wasn't interested in her. If anything, he hated her. He certainly hadn't taken this case for her sake. Yet it was painfully obvious that his taking such a case was an extraordinary occurrence—a waste of his valuable time and specialist knowledge.

And he wasn't even getting properly paid for it! A thousand dollars couldn't possibly cover everything: the time he had spent finding the Seftons and getting their testimony—his contemptuous scorn at her suggestion that they were paid witnesses demolished any doubt on that score—plus the time he had spent with her. And now arguing her case in court.

So it had to be what he'd said it was—a matter of personal honour! Proving something to himself—or more likely proving something to her. It was totally confusing!

Elizabeth didn't have time to ponder the matter further. The case was called by the clerk, and proceedings got under way.

The police sergeant who had questioned Elizabeth gave his evidence first, reading from notes he had taken at the scene of the accident, and from his visit to the defendant. Elizabeth seethed with outrage when he failed to mention the boy on the bicycle, but she had to admire the deft way in which Price Domenico forced out the cogent points in cross-examination.

Neither she nor the Seftons were the least bit shaken in their evidence, but she realised how very well Price Domenico covered all the ground before handing them over to the other barrister. The opposition didn't have a leg left to stand on.

The truth was so patently obvious that the prosecution limply let the case go. The magistrate had a few scathing things to say about the police investigation before benevolently declaring Elizabeth Mary Alexandra Kent innocent of the charge, and commending her for her bravery in risking her own life to save a child's.

Elizabeth thanked the Seftons for their testimony, and the trouble they had gone to in order to give it. She could accept that the Sefton family was only too pleased to have been of help to her. Their son was alive and well. But Price Domenico's motive for helping her was still completely obscure. And intensely disturbing.

Even though justice had finally been done, Elizabeth felt little satisfaction in her exoneration. She was consumed with guilt over all the things she had said to the man who had proved her innocence—fairly, and at great cost to himself!

The Seftons finally took their leave in the corridor outside the courtroom. Elizabeth turned to Price Domenico, knowing what she had to do, but not how to do it. His eyes bored into hers, hard and faintly mocking.

'Your slate is now wiped squeaky clean, Miss Kent. I doubt that you will grant me the same exoneration, but I hope you'll think twice before leaping to conclusions in future.'

Elizabeth swallowed hard and forced the necessary words out. 'Mr Domenico, I don't understand why you chose to do what you've done, but——'

'No. You wouldn't!' he retorted savagely. 'I'm sure this is the very first slur ever cast on your pristine person. It's not the first cast on mine. And I resent it fiercely. I resent it even more fiercely when it's delivered by my son's schoolteacher.'

She stared up at him, seeing the steely pride that was bent on inflicting wound for wound. And the words he had spoken to the magistrate echoed accusingly in her ears—*a matter of personal honour*.

'You owe me a fee, Miss Kent,' he reminded her. 'For proving your innocence beyond all reasonable doubt.'

She shook her head in wretched dismay as she opened her handbag and took out the envelope. 'It's not enough.' Her eyes accused him of deceiving her.

'You know it's not enough for all you've done. You knew all along it wouldn't be.'

'We agreed on an amount. That's all that's necessary,' he said, taking the envelope from her trembling fingers and sliding it into an inside coat pocket.

Elizabeth couldn't let the matter rest, not when she had been so wrong about everything. 'Please...send me an account of all your expenses. I'll pay it off. Every month I'll give you all I can.'

His eyes glittered with some intense satisfaction. 'You've paid...what I wanted you to pay, Miss Kent. For the rest, I prefer to leave people like you in my debt. You owe me something which is worth far more than money. And don't think for one moment that I'll ever forget it—or let you forget it.'

'What do you mean, people like me?' Elizabeth asked in bewilderment.

He swept her up and down with a look of bitter derision. 'The well-bred class, Miss Kent. The kind who would only come to a low-life type like me as a last resort. The kind who would expect me to be honoured to do their dirty business for them, but deny me the courtesy of any respect or social equity. The kind who wouldn't even allow me the normal interest of a parent meeting his son's teacher for the first time. The kind who throw mud, and no matter how many times I wash it away, no matter how much I do to demonstrate my innocence of any wrongdoing, they just keep on throwing more stinking mud.'

He gave her a mocking salute. 'Well, here's mud in your eye, Miss Kent! And a good day to you!'

He strode off, leaving her so shattered that any positive reaction was totally undermined. The headmaster's words jabbed out of her memory—in a stand-up fight Price Domenico would tear his opponent to shreds. And that was what he had just done to her.

But he was wrong about what kind of person she was. Obviously she had made a terrible mistake in thinking him a criminal like his father, but to dump her in the same class as a Mrs Wetherington-Jones was simply not the truth!

Her own pride propelled her forward, and she didn't care what anyone else thought as she ran down the corridor after Price Domenico.

'Wait!' she called, uncaring of her dignity, uncaring of anything else but proving she wasn't the only one who had been wrong.

He didn't pause in his step. He went right on striding as if he disdained to acknowledge her very existence. Which only made Elizabeth more determined to catch him and stop him in his tracks. She wouldn't allow him to spurn her like a dog that had dirtied his path. Even if she *was* stupid. She caught the sleeve of his gown and hung on with all the mad obsessiveness of a bull-terrier.

He swung on her, eyes blazing. 'What the hell do you think you're doing?'

'If you take another step... I'll damn well tackle you!' Elizabeth panted back at him, every bit as fiercely antagonistic as her quarry.

He faced her with supreme contempt. 'What more can I do for you?'

'Accept my apology,' Elizabeth bit out grimly. 'I might be guilty of leaping to false conclusions, but I wasn't the first to start casting stones. You have a fine line in prejudice yourself! And I've had twenty-two years of self-styled superior men telling me that I'm something that I'm not. I'm not going to take that any more. Not from you or anyone else. But I am sorry...for what I thought about you...for accepting what other people believe.'

The flicker of surprise in his eyes gave her a fierce elation. She plunged on, clawing away at his victory over her. 'I will not be indebted to you. Not morally, not financially, not in any way whatsoever. If you won't accept what I'm offering...what I can give...then I owe you nothing. But you do have my heartfelt gratitude...' however much it hurt her to say it, she forced the words out '...and I'm sorry I was so stupid.'

His expression eased from hostility to one of weighing reserve. 'If I'm so wrong about you, Miss Kent, you can wipe off your debt to me in one stroke. And I will acknowledge any prejudice on my part with an apology.'

Elizabeth was instantly wary. Knowing now how tricky he could be, she was not about to be sucked into another dreadful mistake. 'Do I have to trust you?' she asked suspiciously.

'No more than I have to trust you. You may accede to my demand or ignore it.'

'What demand?'

A weary cynicism settled in his eyes. 'You believed—because of my father's associations—like father, like son. Perhaps it's true in many ways. I don't disown my father—whatever he did. In his own lights, he did what he had to do in order to survive. And he had his own code—family first.'

A glitter of intense pride diffused the cynicism. 'And let me tell you something, Miss Kent. For all your slurs on my father, as far as I'm concerned, he was a better person than you are. A better person than anyone else I have ever met.'

The wounding words forced Elizabeth back behind a shield of cool dignity. 'You might be right, Mr Domenico. I cannot judge, since I did not know your father, or what drove him to do what he did—any more than you know me. However, if you would come to your demand...'

His mouth tightened into a grim line. 'You will never cast any slur on my father again!'

'That's all you want?' Elizabeth questioned, unable to believe there was not some other rider to his request. 'I owe you thousands of dollars...'

'It's worth more than money to me, Miss Kent!' he snapped.

For several long moments they stared into each other's eyes, locked in an elemental battle of wills that was charged with so much electric tension that Elizabeth felt as if every cell in her body was tingling...every sense heightened to an extraordinary awareness.

She could hear her own heart thumping, feel her skin begin to prickle with goose-bumps, smell the slight mustiness of his barrister's wig, taste the bitterness of both their lives, see the faint dilation of his pupils as he bored his challenge to the very core of her soul.

'I know—very well—that there are some things worth more than money, Mr Domenico. So I accept,' she said with quiet dignity. 'I'd be obliged if you would accept something from me.'

Impatient rejection flicked over his face. 'I told you——'

'I'm inviting you to lunch with me . . . now . . . if you're not tied up with any other matter. I owe you something. I want to repay it . . . however inadequately. And unless you want to eat your words about me, Mr Domenico, you'll accept.'

Disbelief was quickly followed by a mocking scepticism. 'With all due respect for your impulsive invitation, might I advise you to think twice about it? There are other people . . . who disapprove of my so-called criminal associates. The gossip, Miss Kent, think of the gossip—if people believe you are becoming a criminal yourself . . .'

'My invitation stands, Mr Domenico,' Elizabeth said emphatically. 'Take it or leave it. Without prejudice. But I would like us to be friends.'

The tawny-yellow eyes glittered with derision. But a crooked little half-smile suggested that he was amused by her determined openness. 'Very well. I accept. I have no objection to lunching with a beautiful woman who would like to be my friend.'

Elizabeth flushed. He made it sound as if she was propositioning him. 'I didn't mean . . .' She bit her lip as she realised that he was taking a malicious pleasure from her confusion. Her chin lifted in automatic pride. 'Where do you usually go for a luncheon date, Mr Domenico?'

His eyes danced with unholy enjoyment. 'Kable's. At the Regent Hotel. But it is rather expensive. If you'd prefer to go somewhere cheaper . . . and safer . . .'

'Kable's it is, then,' Elizabeth said determinedly. If it cost her every cent she had left in her bank account, she would give him the best luncheon the restaurant could provide. Even if it cost more than that, she could sell her video set before the account from her credit card came in.

'We'll catch a taxi...if and when you're ready to leave,' she added quickly.

The amusement in his eyes was replaced by a long hard scrutiny that stretched Elizabeth's nerves to breaking-point. 'Dangerous'...'totally amoral'... the headmaster's words thudded through her mind, conjuring up doubts and fears. But she couldn't take anyone's opinion of Price Domenico on trust any more. Certainly what she had invited was not safe—not safe at all where her mental equilibrium was concerned—but if she didn't go through with it now, she would deserve his contempt.

'I have no more business here and my car is parked nearby,' he said slowly. 'If you don't mind being my passenger...?'

'Thank you. That'll be fine,' she agreed, inwardly relieved to be saving a few dollars, but ready to die before she would show it.

'Then shall we adjourn?' he said with a twist of irony and an invitational wave of his hand. He told himself he was a fool for falling in with her wishes. Her kind invariably stirred the worst in him. Yet there was something about her...

He made no attempt to take her arm. Elizabeth fell into step beside him, her head held high as they walked along. But the silence between them, and the nerve-tingling awareness of the man next to her, forced Elizabeth into an examination of her motives.

It was madness to continue this encounter. There was something about Price Domenico that kept twisting her around, making her feel edgy—incomplete—and her intuition screamed that she was flirting with danger by inviting any further acquaintance with him.

Yet she couldn't bear for him to walk out of her life thinking what he did about her. And it was only a luncheon. The strong feelings he evoked—the power of the man that she found so disturbing—maybe his effect on her would dissipate as she got to know him better.

Besides, she had done him an injustice, and that had to be paid for. An apology wasn't really enough. She had to show him that she meant it. And make him believe her. Why this was so important, Elizabeth didn't stop to consider. But she hoped the luncheon would serve her purpose.

She didn't care how much it cost.

Price Domenico was right.

Some things were worth more than money.

CHAPTER FIVE

ELIZABETH'S feet faltered to a dead halt as Price Domenico went to his car. It was a sleek gold Jaguar XJS. Her whole body tensed as he opened the passenger door for her. After several sickening experiences with her husband, she had vowed never to ride in a sports car again.

'Changed your mind?' Price Domenico softly mocked.

She met his taunting tiger eyes with stubborn belligerence. 'How fast do you drive?'

He frowned. 'Still nervous after your accident?'

'No. Just nervous about people who drive sports cars. I don't enjoy being frightened out of my mind, Mr Domenico. If that's how you get your kicks, I'd rather we take a taxi.'

'I like comfort and good performance, Miss Kent. But rest assured, I keep to the law. We will drive to the Regent at a very sedate pace.' His lip curled sardonically. 'The inner-city traffic hardly allows for more, even if you doubt my word.'

'You don't force your way into traffic-lanes with a burst of aggressive speed? Or feel a need to beat everyone else off the mark when the traffic lights change?' she demanded suspiciously.

'I'll restrain myself,' he replied drily.

'I'm quite likely to throw up if you don't,' she warned.

'I'll keep that in mind.'

Elizabeth forced herself to step into the car. He closed the door after her and she instantly felt the fear that used to grip her in Simon's car. She sternly told herself that it was utterly unreasonable, and tried to calm her nerves by buckling the seat-belt and checking that it was completely secure.

Price Domenico opened his door, removed his barrister's gown and wig, and tossed them on to the back seat. He was wearing a dark grey suit which subtly emphasised his very masculine physique, and Elizabeth couldn't help but think how handsome he looked as he slid on to the seat beside her.

Her pulse fluttered with excitement at the thought of sharing the next hour or so with him. Her wildly irrational sense of anticipation mocked all her good and proper reasons for asking him to lunch with her. And telling herself how stupid such feelings were did not dampen them at all.

He leaned forward, slotted in the ignition key and the powerful engine throbbed into life. Despite the assurances she had been given about his driving, Elizabeth could not stop herself from tensing up.

He threw her a sharp look, then eased the car out of its parking place. He did not proceed towards the exit of the private car park, but kept the engine idling as he spoke to her. Gently and rather kindly.

'Who traumatised you over sports cars? Some devil-may-care boyfriend?'

Elizabeth took a deep breath in an effort to relax. 'My husband,' she answered briefly.

Price Domenico did not drive on. Elizabeth suddenly realised he might be thinking that Simon was still very much alive. She looked sharply at him, and flushed at the coldly assessing look in his eyes.

'Does he still frighten you?'

'No,' she replied quickly, and, anxious to clear away the subject, she hastily added, 'He was involved in an accident. He... he didn't survive.'

'I'm sorry.'

'There's no need to be.' Her retort sounded callous even to her own ears, and her cheeks burned even more painfully as she sought to justify her lack of sentiment over the loss of her husband. 'He made my life a living hell,' she blurted out, then wished she hadn't said that, either.

His eyes narrowed. 'I'm sorry about that, too.'

She flashed him a sceptical look and turned her head away. He couldn't mean that. He was just mouthing words. He probably thought she was a hysterical female, given to exaggeration. Only people who had been traumatised by the cruelty of another partner in marriage would ever be able to realise what she had gone through. Everyone of their acquaintance had thought Simon exciting and charming. She had once done so herself. But the façade hadn't lasted beyond the honeymoon.

'Was it a car crash?'

Elizabeth gritted her teeth. She had told him all he needed to know. There was no husband to object to her lunching with another man. She didn't want to remember her marriage, let alone talk about it. And certainly not to Price Domenico.

'No. In a speedboat. It was his final passion,' she said curtly, uncaring how she sounded as long as Price Domenico stopped digging at that miserable part of her past. To make doubly sure, she added, 'Please don't go on about it. My marriage ended five years ago and I——'

'Five years? And you're still hung up about it?' The incredulous note lingered in his voice as he sharply added, 'It was that bad?'

Goaded by the tone of his question, and the implication that he thought she was stupid to be still affected after all this time, Elizabeth's inner bitterness erupted. She swung her head around to face him, her eyes meeting his in glittering challenge.

'Yes, it was that bad! My imperial, chauvinistic husband took over where my father left off. He could do no wrong. Not, at least, in his own eyes. For three years I copped every bit of abuse Simon threw at me. If anything went wrong, it was my fault. I was stupid. I had no guts. I was a snivelling little failure at everything. But the worm finally turned. In the end I learnt to assert myself. And I refused to get on that boat with him the day he died.'

She drew in a shaky breath and tilted her chin in belligerent defiance of anyone's criticism of her. 'I didn't wish him dead, but I can't say I'm sorry. He killed two other innocent people when he lost control of his boat that day. It could have happened in his sports car a dozen times with the kind of risks he took. He had no right to——'

She suddenly realised how much she was pouring out, and snapped herself back under control. 'You can make what you like of that, Mr Domenico, but I am free and single now, and that's the way I'm going to stay. I've fought too hard to get where I'm at to give up one iota of what I've earned.'

He made no comment. Throughout her whole tirade those watchful tawny-yellow eyes had not left hers, but they revealed nothing of what he thought.

'Are we going to lunch, or have you changed your mind?' Elizabeth demanded, more on edge than ever from having revealed so much about herself. In the last few minutes she had told Price Domenico more about her life than she had told anyone in the last few years, and despite her bravado it made her feel very vulnerable.

He gave that crooked little smile that lent his face a striking attraction. Elizabeth's heart misbehaved itself again.

'Any objections have been distinctly overruled. You're the boss. For today, at least,' he drawled. 'And when you're all on fire like that—I hope you don't mind my saying so—you are very beautiful.'

'You don't mean that,' she said in confused agitation.

'What makes you think I don't mean it?' A glint of sardonic amusement flashed into his eyes.

'The way you say it,' she answered flatly.

'Then I must be saying it wrong.'

The glibness in his voice only emphasised how insincere the compliment was. Elizabeth heaved a deep sigh of frustration. Nothing she had told him made any difference to his opinion of her. He had made up his mind that she was a certain type of person, and he wasn't going to let her prove that his judgement was wrong. Yet it went totally against her grain to leave him with a false image of her.

Her eyes raked the mocking reserve in his, trying to find some crack in his armour. 'Would it hurt so much to put your bias aside for a little while, and accept that I might be sincere in wanting to make amends? Is that too impossible to ask?'

A cynical weariness dragged over his face. 'Miss Kent, all you want is to feel better about what happened between us. So you can then dismiss it from your mind. You've tidied up your life after the mistake you made in your choice of a husband, and now you want to tidy up after the mistake you made with me. And you want me to play along and make it easy for you.'

'And you prefer not to make it easy for me . . . is that it?' she asked. 'Is that the reason you accepted my invitation?'

The unsympathetic glitter in his eyes was answer enough. Resentment burnt over her sense of guilt.

'Do you think it's fair to keep punishing me for something that was mostly your own fault?' she demanded angrily. 'If you hadn't played along with me in your office that afternoon, with all your talk of cash up-front...pretending to be a criminal...if you had denied what I said then, as you did today——'

'You wouldn't have believed me,' he cut in acidly.

'You didn't give me the chance!' she retorted fiercely. 'Any more than you're giving me one now. But if it makes you feel better to go ahead and use me as your whipping-boy, then do so. That's nothing new. I've never had anything easy.'

She turned away in bitter disappointment at his intransigent antagonism towards her, and gestured resignedly towards the steering-wheel. 'Let's get on with it. I apologise for the fact that I'm not too good at turning the other cheek when I keep getting hit, but don't let that stop you from enjoying yourself.'

She could feel his gaze boring into her, but she stared stubbornly ahead, too proud to beg any more from him, and too miserable to do anything else but retreat inside herself.

She barely noticed when the car started to move forward. There was no loud revving of the engine or quick acceleration; he drove with careful smoothness. It demonstrated a consideration that Elizabeth no longer expected from him, or from anyone else, but she was grateful for it. She was in a nervous mess as it was. She certainly didn't need any further aggravation.

And the truth was—for all that she prided herself on her fair-mindedness—Price Domenico was probably right. If he had denied being in any way involved in shady rackets that afternoon, Elizabeth was not at all sure that she would have believed him. She had been too prejudiced simply to accept his word for it. More likely than not, she would have thought he was intent on getting rid of her because she wasn't worth his while.

He had dealt her a salutary lesson instead. And the depth of his personal outrage could be measured by the time and trouble and cost he had gone to in order to ram the lesson home. But did he have to keep on being so vengeful about her blunder? Couldn't he see that she was sincerely sorry for having been so misguided?

Perhaps she should try to be more understanding—look at it from his point of view. He had said she wasn't the first to cast a slur on him because of his father. He had probably been subjected to such slurs all his life—the kind that Mrs Wetherington-Jones put on Ricky. It must be extremely difficult to put up with being automatically cast as a bad character and an undesirable associate. Aggravating. Impossible.

A lot worse than being called stupid.

She was letting this encounter go all wrong, letting him needle her. The wiser course—indeed, the only right course—was to be sympathetic and appeasing.

Although that wasn't likely to work, either, given his approach towards her. And how was she supposed to change that when he was so sceptical of everything she said? He was impossible. The situation was impossible. There was only one positive thing she could count on from his acceptance of her invitation—no matter if the luncheon turned into a total fiasco, at least she had made some gesture of atonement.

However, that thought gave her little consolation. What she really wanted was Price Domenico's forgiveness. His approval and respect. And also... Elizabeth's mind whirled into confusion as other, more indefinable feelings crowded out all sensible reasoning. She made a valiant attempt at pushing them aside as the car turned on to a ramp which led up to the hotel entrance.

Elizabeth had never been inside the Regent Hotel, but she knew it was one of the premier hotels in Sydney. One look at the foyer was enough to tell her that anything here was going to be hideously expensive. At the prices they would charge, she would probably end up choking on every mouthful of food, she thought glumly. But the die was cast, so she had to put the best possible face on it.

Even before the car came to a halt, a smartly uniformed concierge was moving towards it. He opened Elizabeth's door and she quickly alighted. Price Domenico left the car in the care of another hotel employee, who drove it down a private ramp, presumably to a basement parking area. The whole atmosphere was one of style.

Elizabeth was relieved that she had worn her best suit as she eyed the people strolling around the huge foyer. Everyone looked to be dressed in high fashion, which was only to be expected at such a place.

Price Domenico joined her on the footpath. 'Safe and sound?' he murmured derisively, scanning her face for any signs of strain.

'Yes. Thank you,' she said stiffly. His manner made it difficult, but she forced herself to carry through her resolution. 'I'm sorry I made such a fuss about the car. And for getting angry with you.'

'Don't worry. You were quite right. I *was* making you a whipping-boy for a lot of things you weren't responsible for.' His mouth quirked into an ironic smile. 'Call it the straw that broke the camel's back and you wouldn't be too far wrong.'

Relief broke through her enforced restraint and she replied with a burst of heartfelt truth. 'One way or another, I've had a fair acquaintance with a lot of straws too, Mr Domenico. I regret very much that I laid that one on you. But I'm glad you threw it back in my face today. Justice might be a bad joke, but I'd rather see it served than not.'

He gave her a long, considering look that had none of the cynicism or mockery he had directed at her before. 'Perhaps we can serve it better over lunch,' he said, and stepped over to one of the entrance doors to hold it open for her.

He had relented. He was going to give her a chance. What had pushed him from hostility to a cautious neutrality she did not know, but at least now she could hope that they might reach an understanding. Why that meant so much to her, Elizabeth didn't stop to consider. As she went past him into the grand foyer of the hotel, her spirits soared so high that she gave him a brilliant smile.

She could even enjoy feasting her eyes on the luxurious spaciousness around her. After all, this would probably be a once-in-a-lifetime experience for her, and there was really no point in worrying how much it would cost.

The foyer rose three podium-levels high, and a centrepiece of small trees flourished under a bank of skylights. To the left was a wide and handsome staircase leading to the upper floors. In front of her was an elegant grouping of leather lounges and coffee-tables.

'Miss Kent!'

Elizabeth's head jerked around at the call of her name, all pleasure in her surroundings instantly wiped out. Her heart had caught at the voice—the tone unmistakable—even before her eyes found the woman coming towards her from the reception-desk.

Mrs Wetherington-Jones!

Of all the people she could have run into, it had to be her!

'Fancy seeing you here,' the condescending voice ran on. Then, as Price Domenico stepped towards Elizabeth's side, unmistakably placing himself as her escort, the self-styled arbiter of well-bred society stopped dead in her tracks. Her expression could not have been more shocked and affronted if she'd been faced with an apparition from hell.

Having been guilty of thinking the worst of Price Domenico herself, Elizabeth was all the more motivated to flout this woman's prejudice. Besides which, she could hardly pretend not to be with him. And after what he had done for her, and the promise he had extracted from her regarding his father, it would be like playing Judas to deny him in any way. No matter what trouble it caused her, Elizabeth was not about to take a backward step. She plastered a polite smile on her face and forced her voice into a pleasant matter-of-fact tone.

'How nice to see you, Mrs Wetherington-Jones!' Then, very deliberately, she turned to the man beside her, linked her arm with his, and added, 'Have you met Mr Domenico?'

'I have,' Mrs Wetherington-Jones sniffed.

'Madam,' Price Domenico acknowledged coldly.

'I am surprised at the company you keep, Miss Kent,' Mrs Wetherington-Jones remarked waspishly, transferring her haughtily withering look to Elizabeth.

'I am always pleased to meet the parents of my pupils, Mrs Wetherington-Jones,' Elizabeth replied in blithe disregard for the implied criticism. 'Particularly Mr Domenico. I'm very honoured to have his company for lunch today. In fact, when I asked him I wasn't even sure he would accept.'

A choking sound came from Mrs Wetherington-Jones's throat. Her beady blue eyes shot barbs of bitter disapproval at Elizabeth. 'I hope you know what you're doing, Miss Kent.'

'So do I,' Elizabeth replied, and continued on with determined sang-froid. 'At the present moment, we're on our way to Kable's——'

An apoplectic look made ravages on the well-preserved face. 'I'll take your word for it, Miss Kent,' was the icy interruption. 'Now, if you'll excuse me...'

She swept past them without waiting for a reply. Elizabeth was just as glad to see the back of her. She had never liked Mrs Wetherington-Jones, and liked her even less now. The woman didn't have any manners.

'That was indiscreet of you,' Price Domenico commented, pointedly looking down at the hand on his arm before meeting her eyes with a cold pride that sent shivers down her spine. 'And I do not need a champion,' he grated.

His reproof was like a slap in the face. She hastily removed her hand from his arm, painfully embarrassed by the impulse that had suggested a friendship that didn't exist. And deeply hurt by his rejection. She had only been trying to show him that she stood by her word. Couldn't she do anything right where he was concerned?

'I'm sorry,' she sighed dejectedly.

'Undoubtedly you will be. That woman has bigger claws than you have, and she won't hesitate to use them. She's on the school-board at Alpha Academy. So watch your back, Miss Kent.'

Elizabeth grimaced, all too aware of the influence Mrs Wetherington-Jones could wield. But she still didn't regret standing up to her, even though Price Domenico resented the way she had done it. 'I can look after myself,' she said, determined not to buckle under any kind of tyranny.

He frowned. 'If you get into trouble, let me know.'

'I don't need a champion, either,' she flashed at him in proud independence.

And for the first time she saw a look of respect, even a grudging admiration in his eyes. 'No. I don't think you do,' he said quietly.

Elizabeth flushed with a silly feeling of pleasure. He was a terribly unsettling person, but she really did want to leave him with a good opinion of her. Hoping to avoid any further gaffe, she said, 'I'm afraid you'll have to lead the way here. I don't know where Kable's is.'

He nodded towards the wide granite staircase that was set off so elegantly with gleaming brass banisters. Then, with a deliberation that cancelled his former rejection, he picked up her hand and tucked it around his arm.

'It's only one flight up. Let's see if we can manage without the elevator,' he said with a dry whimsy that was very close to being friendly.

Elizabeth chided herself for the optimistic feeling which Price Domenico had already shattered twice in the short time they had been together since leaving the court-house. Being with him was like picking her way over a minefield, yet there was a heady exultation in finding herself safe on the other side. Even if it was only a temporary haven before setting out on the next foray into the unknown.

Her palm tingled where it rested on his coat-sleeve, aware of the muscular forearm beneath the fine wool. He matched his step to hers in an unobtrusive, companionable way. Elizabeth was warmed by a sense of togetherness—probably more wish than reality—and it was a foolish, dangerous fantasy.

Her gaze was drawn to his profile, trying to see what it was about him that affected her so deeply. Almost in the same instant he glanced down at her, their eyes meeting sharply, and again that unnerving impact shook her. He jerked his face forward. His step didn't miss a beat. But he had felt it, too! However quickly and determinedly he covered up, she was almost sure he had experienced the same magnetic pull of attraction!

Every instinct, every intuitive sense she had, beat out a loud warning that she was indeed moving into unknown territory with each further step she took with this man. Yet the temptation to go on was irresistible.

CHAPTER SIX

PRICE DOMENICO was certainly known at Kable's. He was greeted by name. Without any discussion at all, he and Elizabeth were ushered to one of the semi-circular booths set along one side of the elegant restaurant. It afforded more privacy than the open arrangement of tables, and also engendered a sense of intimacy that did nothing to calm Elizabeth's wild thoughts.

A waiter swooped down on them with champagne cocktails that they hadn't even ordered. Price Domenico accepted his as a matter of course, so Elizabeth did the same, although it started her wondering what on earth she had let herself in for.

It worried her further when the menu she was handed had no prices written on it. That almost certainly meant that the prices were astronomical. But she couldn't very well ask for a more informative one without showing she was concerned about the cost. And, in any event, the probability was that every dish was hideously expensive. She might as well stop worrying about saving money on her own meal, and try to enjoy it no matter how extravagant it was.

The wine-list put her head in a spin. Initially it was handed to Price Domenico. He passed it to her in deference to the fact that she was paying for the luncheon. She couldn't see anything under forty dollars a bottle, and had no idea if the cheapest wine was any good or not. Her pride insisted that she couldn't offer him anything of inferior quality, and with a sinking feeling in her stomach she offered it back to him.

'Please...I'm not very knowledgeable about wines, and I want you to have what you'd like. Would you be kind enough to choose?'

Whether he sensed her anxiety or it showed in her eyes, Elizabeth didn't know, but after a moment's pause he smiled at her, and it was almost kindly. 'Unless you want to drink most of a bottle yourself, there's little point in ordering one. I don't drink much when I'm driving.' He nodded towards his cocktail. 'One of these is all I usually have at lunchtime.'

Elizabeth's answering smile was full of relief. 'Then that will be fine for me, too.'

His eyes lingered on her face for several moments before dropping once more to the menu, and Elizabeth was conscious of a very tight feeling in her chest, until she remembered to breathe out. Even then she didn't focus on the list of food she was supposed to be reading. For a few more moments her mind was full of wayward thoughts. Did he truly think her beautiful? Did he find her as attractive as she found him? What had *his* marriage been like?

The waiter came back to take their orders. With their respective meals settled all distractions were removed, and Elizabeth and Price Domenico were left facing each other in solitary silence. In a desperate search for some topic to break the ice, Elizabeth recalled that her failure to respond to his interest in his son had been listed as a black mark against her.

'Would you like to talk about Ricky?' she asked tentatively.

His ironic smile acknowledged her attempt to make amends. 'I know you treat him fairly. More than fairly, if his claim to being your pet is true.'

Elizabeth gave an embarrassed laugh. 'Ricky is one of the most likeable children in my class. But I don't play favourites. One of my least likeable pupils started calling him the teacher's pet out of spite, because he didn't show her the attention she wanted. All the girls tend to vie for his attention. He's very popular.'

'From what I gather, there's only one person's attention he wants. Your name continually peppers his conversation, with or without my encouragement.' He paused, then added, 'I make no apology for pumping Ricky about you. It concerned me that your attitude to him might be prejudiced by what you thought of me. I was relieved that, if it did have any bearing at all, it wasn't apparent to Ricky.'

Shame brought a wave of colour to her cheeks. 'It had no bearing on what I thought of Ricky. He is . . . very sweet . . . lovable . . .'

'Unlike the father,' came the dry response.

Elizabeth wasn't sure if the glitter in his eyes was teasing or taunting. 'You must be a good father,' she said warily. 'For an only child, Ricky is remarkably unspoilt.'

His lips curled in sardonic appreciation. 'Thank you. I try. Unfortunately I don't quite take the place of a mother. Ricky was only one year old when my wife died, and no matter what I do to make it up to him for that loss, I know he feels deprived.'

The mention of his wife stirred a host of questions in Elizabeth's mind, all clamouring to be answered. She was apprehensive about his reaction to any probing of his private life. But he had asked her about her husband.

'Do you still miss her... your wife?' she asked awkwardly, half expecting him to start tearing her to shreds again, and ready to beat a mollifying retreat.

His face tightened a little, and his eyes hardened before he dropped his gaze to the champagne cocktail. For several seconds he turned the glass around on the table without picking it up. 'I'll always remember her,' he said softly.

Then his gaze flicked up to fasten on to Elizabeth's. 'She should not have died as she did. I'll always regret what happened to her. And always wish I had been at her side... when she needed me most.'

The glimpse of pain in his eyes should have warned Elizabeth to leave the subject alone, but she felt driven to know more. 'I heard... is it true... that your wife died of a drug overdose?'

'That was the official report,' he drawled, then with acid bitterness he added, 'No doubt you heard the rest, too. The law swallowed it, and so did the scandal-loving public. But the truth, Miss Kent, was that Rosalie never touched drugs in her life, and would never have done so. Nor was she the type of woman who would ever have been unfaithful to our marriage, no matter what difficulties we had in our relationship.'

A savage mockery slashed from his eyes. 'Do you want to know what really happened?'

'Yes,' Elizabeth answered unequivocally, unable to leave the position unresolved when he had raised such pointed doubts over the official story.

'My wife . . . was kidnapped . . . and murdered . . . as a warning to my father. He would not countenance drug-dealing in his territory. There was no way of proving a case that would stand up in court. The men responsible were far too clever. My father was distraught over Rosalie's death. Just as distraught over the possible danger to me and Ricky, since he could not—would not—give in to the demands being made on him.'

His voice gathered a harshness that overrode the mockery, revealing how deeply the truth still pained him. 'Gambling casinos, SP bookmaking, night-clubs—he ran all those—but he didn't deal in death. Not by drugs or violence. He begged me to take Ricky out of the country. He wanted us safe while he resolved the situation. He refused to discuss his plans with me—said it was his business and I had to stay clear of it. Otherwise his life had all been for nothing. I didn't know until afterwards that he had contracted terminal cancer and only had six months to live.'

A ragged sigh whispered from his lips and he gave a sad, twisted smile. 'His atonement, he called it, in the letter he left to me. Yet he had nothing to atone. Nothing. It wasn't his fault.'

With a weary shake of his head he relaxed back against the plush padding of the seat, and viewed Elizabeth through hooded eyes. He spoke in a completely flat voice, without life or expression.

'My father had never killed anyone. Nor ordered anyone to be killed. But he went out and shot the ringleaders who had planned and ordered Rosalie's kidnap and murder. He was shot dead in return. And that, Miss Kent, is the truth about my wife's death . . . and my father's.'

His background was so full of grief and pain that it wrenched her heart to think of what they had all been through—Rosalie, Price, his father. No wonder he had been so savage with her for having spoken of his father in demeaning terms. And it more than explained his cynicism about the legal system—justice, an ideal we like to dream about, but more often than not a bad joke.

And she had gone to him, outraged by a false charge of negligent driving! An insignificant molehill against the mountain he had been faced with.

She searched for something to say to him, but everything seemed hopelessly inadequate. She shook her head, distressed that there was nothing she could offer but her sympathy. 'Thank you for telling me,' she said huskily. 'It must have been a very difficult time for you. I don't know . . . how you bore it.'

'By doing what my father wanted me to do. And one of those things was fighting for justice on the right side of the law.' He gave an ironic little smile. 'Which I wanted to show you today.'

'I'm glad you did.'

'I believe you,' he said with the first touch of warmth.

Elizabeth felt the same relief and satisfaction as she did when she had gained a credit in a particularly testing examination. Price Domenico was a hard marker—justifiably so, considering all he had suffered—and his belated acknowledgement of her sincerity fed her hope of reaching an even better understanding with him.

Their starters were served. Elizabeth ate the lobster tails she had ordered with good appetite, forgetting all about the cost in her eager anticipation for more companionable conversation with Price Domenico.

The plates were cleared away.

Another awkward silence ensued.

Price Domenico sipped at his drink, looking totally withdrawn in private thought.

Elizabeth was once more racked to find a subject that would be painless, but would tell her more about him. She hadn't come up with anything when he put down his glass and leaned forward, resting his forearms on the table as his gaze lifted and fastened on hers, his eyes intensely watchful.

'I accept that you mean what you say, Miss Kent, but any friendship with me is more a burden than anything else. I give you fair warning—I'm not a desirable person to know, let alone acknowledge as a friend. I'll be even more beyond the social pale in the coming months.'

He paused and there was a sardonic curl of his lips as he added, 'I'm taking on the Hartley case, and the mud will be flying in all directions.'

Elizabeth frowned. 'The Member of Parliament that all the scandal is about?'

'The same.'

'You're defending him?'

'Yes.'

She stared incredulously at him, recalling the charges of drug-dealing and involvement in brothels. She couldn't believe—after all Price had been through—that he would defend anyone who was guilty of drug-dealing.

'You believe he's innocent,' she deduced with intuitive conviction. 'That's why you're taking the case.'

His eyes danced with pleasure, stirring a whole flock of butterflies in Elizabeth's stomach and sending her pulse-rate into overdrive.

'Perhaps, of more consequence, is the right of all people to be adequately represented—particularly in a case where there is such a groundswell of prejudice and bias. Everyone likes to think ill of a politician, and the evidence looks very black against him. Perhaps Hartley is guilty.'

'But you don't think so,' Elizabeth said confidently.

'No,' he said seriously. 'The whole thing smells suspiciously like a frame-up.'

'But why would anyone want to do that?'

His eyes lightly mocked her naïveté. 'I suspect he was doing too well as Minister for Law and Order. It would have cost some people a lot of money. It's easier to remove the disturbing force than withstand an investigation. The pity of it is, even if we clear the mud, his career in politics is ruined. But at least he won't go to jail. Not if I can help it.'

Elizabeth felt depressed by the realities he was stating. 'It's all so unfair, isn't it?' Her eyes flashed with a burst of righteous indignation. 'But that doesn't make you a less desirable person to know.

If he's innocent... I like you all the more for standing up for him.'

He laughed—more a low, throaty chuckle than a laugh—but it warmed Elizabeth right down to her toes. And his eyes—those tawny tiger eyes—lit with a vibrant glow that sizzled every sensible thought out of her mind.

'You are beautiful,' he said in a low intimate voice that curled around her heart. 'And I hope I'm saying it right this time.'

Elizabeth was saved from having to make a reply by the arrival of the main course. The waiter fussed over serving the vegetables and making sure that everything was to their satisfaction before he withdrew.

Elizabeth stared down at the meal she had ordered, not really seeing it, rocked by the realisation that she was responding to Price Domenico in ways and on levels that she had never experienced before. It wasn't simply a physical attraction—although that was becoming alarmingly strong. He was engaging her emotions, making her respond to him. And the mental accord she felt with him went beyond any loyalty to the principles of justice.

Belatedly she picked up her knife and fork and began eating, while her mind turned over what was happening to her. She had said that she wanted to be friends with him. And that was all she wanted. To invite or encourage any other kind of relationship with him would really be stupid.

For one thing, they were too different.

She was a battler.

He was brilliant.

She had vowed never to give any man the kind of power over her life that would reduce her to less than she was. Price Domenico *was* dangerous. Although she had fought back today and earned some respect from him, he could very easily grind her down and make her feel inferior—if he had a mind to.

'Not very enjoyable?'

The question snapped her out of her introspection. 'What do you mean?'

He had finished his trout and was regarding her with quizzical interest. 'The Victorian beef. You seem to be picking at it.'

'No. It's fine! Really fine,' she replied quickly. It was the truth. Although she hadn't appreciated it before, he brought it to her attention. She ate the rest with more concentration, aware that he was watching her intently.

'How long have you been at Alpha Academy?' he asked as she finished her champagne cocktail

'Only this year. I was teaching at a convent school before that,' she supplied, feeling more confident of keeping her equilibrium on this line of conversation.

'Why did you move?'

'For one thing, the salary was higher. And I wanted to see how I would cope with very bright pupils. I plan to teach at high-school level soon. If I pass my exams this year I'll be a Bachelor of Arts,' she said with pride in her achievement.

'You're teaching and studying at the same time?'

She nodded, smiling at his surprise. 'I'm an external student at the University of New England. It's mostly done by correspondence. I'm sent cassettes of lectures. And there are residential schools that I go to in April and September, during the school holidays.'

'That can't leave you with much free time for yourself,' he remarked.

'But it is for myself,' she said, frowning at his failure to comprehend that. 'It's what I want to do. If nothing else, I'm proving to myself that I'm . . .' she bit down on the hateful words which had almost slipped out, and quickly replaced them with others '. . . that I can do it.'

'Is that so important?' he asked softly.

'It is to me,' she asserted, her eyes flashing stubborn commitment to the task.

He nodded. A whimsical smile softened his face. 'You've got guts, Miss Kent. You might sometimes fail at some of the things you set yourself, but I can't see you ever snivelling about it. We all make the occasional human error, but there is one thing you certainly are not. No one could ever fairly accuse you of being stupid.'

His recollection of what she had said about her husband, and his shrewd application of it, stunned Elizabeth into a fast reappraisal of his powers of comprehension. Was she so transparent to him, or was he more perceptive than most people?

'Why did you marry him?' he asked while Elizabeth was still floundering over his quick understanding of her innermost needs.

'Why did you marry your wife?' she retorted sharply, disturbed by the feeling that he was getting too close to her—too close for her to fend him away. Yet the moment the question spilled from her lips, Elizabeth desperately regretted it. After all he had told her—to remind him of such agonising horrors! She writhed in shame, too appalled at her monstrous lack of tact to retrieve the blunder.

But he did not castigate her, nor turn away. There seemed to be an understanding sympathy in his eyes. 'I loved her,' he answered with direct simplicity.

Elizabeth couldn't understand herself. It was crazy for her to feel hurt by those words, but they did hurt. She wished she could know what it would be like to be loved by Price Domenico. To be loved and cherished and needed and wanted...

Simon hadn't loved her. And, though she had fooled herself at the time, she hadn't loved him either. She suddenly felt as if her whole life was hopelessly barren—always would be barren.

'You haven't answered me,' he said quietly.

She raised bleak grey eyes to the golden warmth of his, knowing that for all the pain his family had given him at least he had known love. Still did with his son.

'He was the first person to give me the sense of being loved and wanted,' she replied flatly.

He frowned. 'Not your mother?'

'She died soon after I was born.'

'And your father?'

Elizabeth grimaced. 'He wanted a boy who might have done him proud. I was a stupid girl instead. He approved of Simon, which should have been a red-flag warning to me. Actually it made me feel that I was finally doing something right. Which demonstrates how hopelessly deluded I was. But my father did enjoy having a manly son-in-law. He died a year after Simon and I were married, and he bequeathed what little worldly goods he had to my husband on the principle that men were better suited to handle such things.'

'Did he prove to be better suited?'

Her eyes hardened. 'That is probably a matter of opinion, Mr Domenico. It would not have been my choice to live on an overdraft. And I hope, when I die, I'll do so without owing anyone anything. I don't like being in debt.'

'I see,' he murmured. And again Elizabeth had the churning impression that he saw too much.

A waiter removed their plates, and another waiter wheeled up a sweet-trolley that was loaded with an array of sumptuous temptations. The interruption provided a much-needed respite from Price Domenico's subtle cross-examination.

Although Elizabeth had immediately decided on the strawberry shortcake, she took enough time over her selection to regain the presence of mind to turn the conversation away from herself. The moment the waiter departed she took the initiative.

'You obviously loved your father very much. Would you tell me more about him?'

She sensed his reluctance, saw the weighing wariness in his eyes, and knew that she was treading on very sensitive ground where one wrong reaction or response could shade his present good opinion of her. But she did not retract her request, and, after a few moments' uncertain silence, he decided to trust her with his confidence.

Elizabeth listened with more and more sympathy as the facts slowly unfolded, pruned to the bare bones, but even more telling in their starkness.

His grandparents were displaced people from the Second World War. They emigrated with their family from Italy to Australia. To pay off their passage they had to spend two years in an emigrant camp at Greta, near Cessnock, where there was work in the coal-mine. His grandfather was killed in a mining accident. His grandmother moved the family to Sydney, hoping to get work. There was no employment to be had for her. She hadn't learnt to speak English.

His father, who had only been fourteen at the time, managed to get a job as a runner for an SP bookmaker at the race-courses. He could do sums so fast and accurately that he was soon promoted to handling the books. The family survived on what he earned, but his younger brother contracted poliomyelitis. There were huge medical bills. To raise the money needed, Joe Domenico started his first illegal venture in gambling—a two-up game that he operated wherever he could gather enough customers.

He was smart and he ran a straight game. His reputation grew among the gambling fraternity, and opportunities to expand his operations were offered. Although what he did was illegal, he figured it wasn't hurting anyone. Gamblers were gamblers of their own free will, and if they had money to lose, he could employ it for better purposes.

He began making a lot of money. His mother was very unhappy in Australia. She couldn't get used to the language or the customs. Eventually he could afford to send the whole family back to Italy and maintain them with a comfortable living there.

He married an Australian girl, the daughter of a racehorse-trainer. They only had the one child. Price's mother died in a riding accident on her father's property, and Joe Domenico never looked at another woman. He became obsessed with making sure that his son had every advantage, the best education at the best schools, every opportunity to become a respectable pillar of society.

He never forgot his own family's struggle to survive; no man, woman or child ever came to him in need and was turned away empty-handed. He invariably employed people who were down on their luck. When he died he had one of the biggest funerals Sydney had ever seen, not because he was a Godfather in the criminal sense of the word, but because of his beneficence to countless people and charities.

'Unfortunately, his ambitions for me will never be realised,' Price finished sadly. 'I'm respected well enough in legal circles, but the manner of Rosalie's death—and my father's—ensures that I will never be accepted as a pillar of society.'

The world-weary cynicism crept back into his eyes. 'It isn't important to me. What I see of the pillars of society hardly inspires any wish to be counted as one of them. But, for the sake of my father's dreams, I do what I can to give Ricky the best possible chance to climb whatever ladder he sets his sights on.'

Elizabeth smiled in soft sympathy. 'I guess most parents try to do that for their children. But Ricky's very strong-minded, you know. He'll be like you—despising hypocrisy and injustice, and treading his own path regardless of what anyone else thinks.'

Price laughed, his whole face lightening with pleasure, and the laugh subsided into a smile that completely devastated all Elizabeth's well-reasoned resolutions about him. It was utterly impossible to divorce herself from the strong attraction he held for her. Common sense was crushed beneath something far more powerful.

Their coffee had been served and drunk and their cups topped up again while Price had talked about his father's life. The bill for the luncheon was discreetly presented to him as Elizabeth struggled to come to terms with feelings that went beyond all her previous experience.

Price had taken out his wallet before she managed to seize some control of herself. 'No. It's mine,' she said in considerable agitation, and reached for the plate on which the docket lay.

A strong warm hand arrested hers, and the tawny-yellow eyes caressed any resistance into tremulous submission as he answered her objection with persuasive command.

'Allow me—as an apology to you. I was wrong, and it has given me much pleasure to discover how wrong I was about you, Elizabeth. Let this be my atonement for undeserved prejudice.'

His use of her first name plunged Elizabeth further into emotional confusion, and the sensuous stroke of his fingers across her wrist stirred feelings that she had no way of controlling.

'If... if that's what you want,' she said huskily, surrendering to his will without argument because she didn't have the strength of mind to argue.

He withdrew his disturbing touch and produced a credit card. The waiter reappeared at his signal, supplied a pen for the necessary signature, and the whole business was settled before Elizabeth could have second thoughts.

'I'm not sure I feel right about this,' she murmured distractedly.

'You'd prefer me to keep calling you Miss Kent?'

'No. I mean...'

'The lunch?' His mouth curled in self-mockery. 'I meant to make you pay through the nose in every way I could, Elizabeth. It behoves me to pay penance for my sins.'

The curl extended to a charming smile that did nothing to restore her equilibrium. 'If you have nothing else on your agenda, may I offer you a lift home? I promise you, my driving will not cause you any alarm.'

'But... don't you have to go... or be somewhere else?'

'Not with any urgency. I organised free time to coincide with Ricky's school holidays. Yours was the only case that necessitated an interruption to our vacation at Noosa, where Ricky and I both enjoy the relaxed atmosphere of the tropics. I flew down from Brisbane this morning and my return flight isn't until this evening.'

'I'm sorry,' she said, mortified at having dragged him away from a holiday—at even more expense.

'Don't be. I'm not.'

He rose from the table, prompting Elizabeth to join him. She hadn't formally accepted his offer of a lift home, but to refuse seemed out of the question. It wasn't as if she had any other plans. And he had proved himself a careful and considerate driver. Not to accept would be positively churlish, after he had gone to so much trouble on her behalf. Besides, what harm could there be in a twenty-minute car trip together?

He took her arm and tucked it around his, just as he had done in the foyer, but somehow there was something far more intimate about it this time. He smiled at her again, and she felt her own mouth respond automatically. Her whole body responded. And the warning bells that rang somewhere in the back of her mind sounded very distant...insignificant...as they walked off together.

CHAPTER SEVEN

'THAT is where you live?'

The slight sharpness in the question scraped across Elizabeth's taut nerves. Apart from asking for directions when they reached Chatswood, Price Domenico had not instigated any conversation since they had left the Regent Hotel. Neither had Elizabeth. And the silence between them—in the close confinement of the sports car—had heightened her awareness of the man sitting next to her to such an extent that she couldn't even recollect the trip out to her suburb, let alone make any critical comments on his driving.

She looked at the unattractive façade of the old red-bricked apartment-block—no balconies or any structural frills to give some style; no front yard to lend itself to any clever landscaping; not even a front porch leading off from the main entrance. The building had been designed to get a maximum return for minimum outlay.

She swung her gaze back to Price Domenico. His frown rattled her pride. Obviously his home made hers look like a slum. 'It suits me very well,' she bit out coldly.

'No. It doesn't,' he retorted, and the frown was menacing. 'But appearances can be deceptive.'

He opened his door and was out and around the car while Elizabeth was still digesting that last muttered remark. What had he expected? He couldn't still be under the delusion that she came from a wealthy family...could he?

She was slow to alight when he opened her door. She wasn't sure how to handle the situation. But Price Domenico was in no doubt at all. He closed the car door, took her arm, and without the slightest hesitation swept her along with him into the apartment-block.

'No elevator?' he asked as they headed towards the stairwell.

'No. There are only three floors,' Elizabeth excused, feeling more and more conscious of the cheap drabness of the place.

'Where are you situated?'

'At the top.'

Elizabeth halted at the bottom of the bare concrete staircase, hopelessly agitated by the sense of purpose that emanated from him. 'Please...don't feel obliged to see me to my door. It was very kind of you to bring me home.'

The tawny-yellow eyes burned straight through the emotional confusion in her appeal. 'It wasn't kind, Elizabeth. And I don't feel obliged to see you to your door. I want to. And I'm going to do exactly that!'

She didn't ask the obvious question of why. Her mouth had gone completely dry. Her mind was bombarded by wild, chaotic thoughts that she couldn't really credit—or was too frightened to accept. Yet the look in his eyes tugged at the strange alien feelings that were twisting her insides into knots. It did more than that. It compelled an acknowledgement that she didn't want to stop now either...didn't want to turn him away...didn't want to miss out on what might happen if they stayed together a little while longer.

She turned and clattered blindly up the stairs, Price Domenico following one step behind. And it wasn't fear pounding through her heart, Elizabeth realised, but excitement—dangerous, compelling excitement that overrode all practical common sense.

Her mind frantically argued that she shouldn't let him into her apartment, that it was better to part now and go their separate ways—that it was stupid, stupid, stupid to get any further involved with a man who was already tearing her carefully ordered world to shreds.

But she reached her door, unlocked it, and made no objection about Price Domenico stepping into her living-room. She shut the door and stood with her back against it, too uncertain of herself and the way she felt to take any initiative in this encounter. She had nothing to be ashamed of, yet as his gaze roamed slowly around her living space, apparently absorbing every detail of how she lived, Elizabeth was shaken by an even worse sense of vulnerability to his opinion.

'Where do you study?' he asked.

'There's a second small bedroom,' she answered, her voice little more than a whisper.

He walked over to the short hallway beyond the kitchenette, and opened the first door. Elizabeth knew she should be outraged by the uninvited invasion of her privacy. She did not understand why she made no move to stop him or protest, but simply stood there watching him stocktake her possessions.

He did not enter the room, but she was all too aware of what he could see from the doorway: the large second-hand desk and the second-hand office-chair, the cheap pine-board bookcases filled to overflowing with books and folders of notes, the two-bar radiator that kept her feet warm through the long cold nights, the electric typewriter which was her one real extravagance, the inexpensive cassette-player that had no pretensions to hi-fi excellence.

He shook his head and turned back to her. His face looked taut—pale—as if something had sickened him. Yet as he walked towards her the expression in his eyes changed—their bleakness sharpening into intense determination.

He paused near the counter which separated the kitchenette from the living-room. He reached inside his suit-coat and withdrew the envelope she had given him at the court-house—the envelope containing a thousand dollars. She watched, mesmerised by the slow deliberation with which he placed it on the counter and left it there.

'You don't owe me anything, Elizabeth,' he said quietly.

A burning rush of blood swept her from head to foot, firing her into action. She jerked away from the door as words poured from her tongue in pained little bursts. 'No! I won't accept it. I don't want your charity. I pay my own way!'

He caught her hand before she could snatch up the envelope and thrust it back at him—caught it and carried it to his chest, forcibly holding it against him with his own. Her eyes flashed a hurt protest and she lifted her other hand to disengage herself from him. It also was caught and pressed into inaction.

'Elizabeth, listen to me!' He spoke with urgent intensity, his eyes commanding her attention. 'It was my choice. Not yours. The money was irrelevant, except in so far as I wanted you to hurt—as I was hurt. But you've wiped that out. We're square now. There's to be no more hurting——'

'No!' She shook her head vehemently. 'It was an agreement. I took up your time. You did what I asked.'

'I could have had you out of my office within five seconds of your arrival,' he argued. 'I almost did. Only one thing stopped me, and it had nothing to do with helping you, Elizabeth.'

And it was there, simmering in those golden eyes... with no shadow of cynicism or reserve to disguise it... constricting her throat... sending a quiver through her heart... curling down to the pit of her stomach...

Elizabeth could not speak. Could not move. He lifted his hands away from hers. One curved around her throat to the nape of her neck. The other softly stroked her cheek. His eyes never left hers, mesmerising with their purposeful glitter, drawing the response he wanted to see. She stared back at him, knowing she couldn't dissemble, knowing what he intended and totally incapable of stopping it.

He tilted her face, gently caressing her chin with his thumb, then slowly, deliberately, he lowered his mouth to hers. The warm touch of his lips sent a current of electric excitement through her whole body, forcing the release of her breath in a sharp gasp. She heard him make some harsh sound in his throat, then his lips closed more firmly over hers, coaxing her response with a sensuality that was totally compelling. Her lips parted to the soft, tantalising pressure of his mouth and he deepened his kiss.

Elizabeth melted against his strength, any thought of resistance gone. She relaxed in his embrace, her hands curling weakly against his chest as he gathered her closer to him. She felt as if she had never really been kissed before, as if she'd been starved of all that was possible between a man and a woman... what he was showing her, arousing in her, needs that had been dormant which were now shockingly awakened, clamouring to be explored and satisfied.

A little moan of distress whispered from her throat as he withdrew the enthralling intimacy, his lips moving gently, lightly over hers before lifting away. Elizabeth opened her eyes and stared up at him, her mind swirling with a hazy aftermath of unexpected pleasure.

'I've been wanting to do that ever since I first saw you,' he said, his voice low and gravelly, raising goose-bumps down her spine. 'Even when I thought you weren't worth my consideration, I didn't want to let you go. And when I despised you, I wanted to grind you down so hard that you would never forget me. But no matter what I told myself about you, there was still this desire gnawing inside me...'

His hand stroked softly up her cheek, over her hair. His fingers felt for the pins that held her plaited coronet in place.

'I wondered what you would look like with your hair untwined, falling around your shoulders...'

He needed both hands to remove the rubber bands at either end of the thick plait, and he lifted his gaze from hers to focus on the task. Elizabeth found herself staring at his chin, the tanned column of his throat, the white shirt where his suit-coat had fallen open, where her hands lay curled.

Her mind moved sluggishly to encompass the situation. She ought to stop him, it told her, but without much conviction. Hadn't she wanted this all along—to know what it would be like to be kissed by him? To know . . . more?

He wasn't doing anything wrong in letting down her hair. And then he would kiss her again. Her mouth felt full and swollen with tingling sensitivity, wanting the explosive excitement of his experienced sensuality, wanting . . .

But what if he didn't stop there?

His fingers were gently parting the thick swathes of her hair, raking through the long silky tresses, fanning the rippling waves into wild disarray. It was a subtle, insidious attack on the constraint and discipline that had characterised her life for so long—so terribly, achingly long.

But it was dangerous, her mind shrieked. And fear slithered through the drugging fascination of his touch. She forced her hands to uncurl, to spread against his chest for leverage in order to push away. The warmth of his firm flesh infiltrated the fine fabric. The quick hammer of his heart beat under her open palm, sending another weakening wave of excitement through her.

'Elizabeth . . .'

Her name came thickly from his throat. She looked up. The molten gold of his gaze seemed to turn her bones to a heavy, listless treacle. His hands dropped to the waist-button which held the form-fitting line of her suit-coat. A nagging sense of self-preservation insisted she drag her own hands from him to make some token protest against what he was doing. Her fingers fumbled over his, ineffective in stopping their purpose.

He pushed the coat from her shoulders, pulled it slowly down her arms, and the weak urge to resist disintegrated under the persuasive caress of his touch.

'You are so exquisitely feminine,' he murmured, his hands stroking over the curve of her hips, spanning her small waist, sliding up the slippery silk of her blouse, curving around the underswell of her breasts. His thumbs brushed over the soft peaks and began a gentle circling movement, and not for a moment did his eyes release hers, compelling submission with the burning intensity of his desire.

'You didn't want to let me go either, did you?' he said, his voice a low hypnotic whisper.

She felt her nipples harden and jut forward in tingling response. Her blood seemed to rush through her veins with a new, heavy warmth.

'That's why you came after me at the courthouse...why you asked me to lunch with you...why you hung on despite all I said to you. It wasn't only to prove you were not what I thought you were, was it, Elizabeth?'

He spoke with mesmerising certainty, and the apparent detachment with which his hands continued their seductive caresses while he invaded her mind with his words both frightened her and heightened the excitement of the intimacies he was forging . . . claiming . . . insisting upon.

'Beyond the pride and the passionate defence of yourself, there was this.' His voice seemed to throb through her head, closing out any thoughts but the ones he was putting there. 'Beyond my pride and contempt for all you seemed to stand for, there was this. An overwhelming attraction—too strong to deny. That's the truth, isn't it?'

'Yes,' she whispered, forced into the admission because it was the truth.

'There's no longer any need—or reason—for either of us not to be honest about wanting each other now . . . is there?'

His hands slid over her breasts to the base of her throat, to the ruffled tie of her blouse.

'Price . . .' His name burst from her lips, a husky plea—a tremulous protest.

'No, don't say anything. Let me . . .' His voice thickened. 'I want to touch you . . . you want me to . . . I know I'm right.'

She couldn't think. Her whole body trembled as he parted her blouse and his fingers grazed softly down her throat, down her bared skin to the low satin edge of her petticoat. She breathed in quick shallow sips of air, her throat too constricted to cope with more. The pulse-beat from her heart grew faster, stronger, clouding any attempt at coherent thought.

What was right? What was wrong? How far should she let him touch her?

Then his mouth claimed hers again, blotting out all questions, igniting a fiercely wanton response that did not acknowledge any limitations. His hands slid down to her waist, to the pit of her back, drawing her towards him, closer, closer. Her breasts rubbed up against the warm strength of his chest. She clutched at the hard muscles of his upper arms—so firm and taut—aggressively masculine. His fingers stroked downwards, gripping, arching her against him full length so that she felt the aroused thrust of his manhood.

A deep, ragged sigh whispered from his lips and warmed her cheek as he moved his mouth from hers. 'I haven't felt like this for so long. Say it's the same for you, Elizabeth,' he murmured, burying his face in her hair, trailing kisses down her throat.

She couldn't speak. She had never felt like this. Not with Simon...or anyone else...ever! An almost agonising sweetness was coursing through her body. An incoherent cry of desire erupted from her lips as his mouth moved to the soft swell of her breasts. She clutched at his head, her fingers tangling in the black curls. Her legs quivered, too weak to move from the strong support of his thighs.

He bent and lifted her off her feet, cradling her tightly, possessively, in his arms. Elizabeth was only dimly conscious of him carrying her into her bedroom, but when he laid her on the pillows the reality of what was happening jerked at her dazed mind. She tried to focus on it, tried to grope through the insanity of the desire that was engulfing her.

He stroked her hair, spraying it out around her face. His face was taut, intent. His eyes were glittering with an exultant triumph—beyond pleasure and need and desire. He straightened and shed his clothes with careless haste, his eyes on her the whole time, watching, compelling her acquiescence.

Fear surged through Elizabeth at the rampant maleness of his body; the strong, hard planes of it, the dark hair shadowing his chest and loins, the powerful strength of his thighs. She could not appreciate the physical beauty of line and proportion. She saw the animal threat of him.

The madness of what she was doing burst through her mind like a blinding light. He would hurt her! Take her and use her like Simon had. She shuddered and shrank away from him, her limbs barely responding to the rejection her mind screamed for. 'No!' she choked out, shaking her head in helpless agitation. 'I don't want...'

The bed dipped under his weight, spilling her towards him. 'Elizabeth...' His eyes burned into hers. His fingers feathered tenderly across her cheek. 'I won't hurt you...'

She shut her eyelids tight against the power that made chaos of any common sense. She dragged in a shaky breath, fighting the temptation to touch his skin, to feel it naked against hers, to find out if it would be different...

'I'm no good at this,' she excused in ragged desperation. 'I'm sorry for frustrating you, but——'

'Let me be the judge of that,' he murmured, brushing his lips sensuously over hers, cutting off any more words with a slow, deliberate escalation of passion that robbed her of all sense but the need he aroused.

'We're going to be together... say it, Elizabeth,' he breathed with a hoarse need that echoed and amplified the primitive beat of intense wanting inside her. He scattered pleading kisses over her face, searing her fears away with a fiery tenderness that stoked the desire to be one with him...without pretence...without inhibition...without thought of tomorrow.

'Yes!' she cried in a plunging rush.

'Don't be afraid,' he murmured. 'I want to touch—and know—all of you. All of you, Elizabeth.'

She didn't answer. There was no reply to make. She had already surrendered her will to his, and it didn't matter what he did. She had consciously, wantonly passed the point of no return. And it would be different. She knew it had to be different with him. Somehow he made it unbelievably, unimaginably different.

He removed her clothes with a gentle delicacy that heightened the exquisite excitement of his caresses and blotted out the thought of embarrassment. She kept her eyes shut, not wanting anything to distract her concentration on the incredible nerve-quivering way he was exploring her body. It might be wrong—it might be madness—but nothing in her life had ever suggested that she could feel what Price Domenico was making her feel.

'Open your eyes.'

She did. The golden glaze of his desire for her swam into her soul, warming it with a wonder she had never known.

'You're beautiful. Don't hide from me. I want to see...to know...'

She touched her fingers to his lips, savouring the sweet taste of his words. Her eyes filled with a plea for understanding that she felt too shy to voice.

'Didn't you ever make love with your husband?' he rasped, his face darkening at her tongue-tied silence.

'He...' it was difficult to answer the question that carried so many critical overtones '...he had sex with me,' she finished limply.

He made a harsh sound of protest and covered her mouth with his own, intent on drawing any pain from her memories and supplanting it with a pleasure that superseded everything else. It was like drowning, dying, being reborn.

He cared about her. He made her feel wanted and valued and important to him.

Her hands found delight in stroking over the muscled strength of his shoulders. Her body strained against his, eagerly seeking the warm tension of his body, inviting the cover of his naked weight, blindly encouraging the power and thrust that would fuse her with him.

Her breasts swelled into his hands and he bent to them, taking first one and then the other into the moist warmth of his mouth, sucking the sensitised nipples with a rhythmic drawing movement that sent shafts of piercing pleasure through her body. His hand slid down to caress the rounded thrust of her hip, then lower, finding the inner softness of her thighs, his fingers gently fondling her until she shivered from the feverish delight of their knowing caress.

She arched up to him in mindless supplication as surge after surge of wild sensation sent shock-waves crashing through her. She was dimly aware that her fingers were raking his back, urging him to lift himself and come to her. But he denied her need, moving lower, making her flesh leap with his kisses, parting her legs with long, coaxing caresses that set them quivering with expectation.

Her blood pulsed with urgency and impatience, then suddenly burst into liquid fire as his lips moved over the most intimate pleasure-places of her body. She writhed up in shock, gripping his hair, crying out at the unbearable intensity of feeling that shook her.

The whole of her womb felt open to him, longing for his possession, but he held her on the edge of nerve-clenching anticipation until she was frantic with desire for him, calling his name, begging. And at last he came to her, surging into the aching emptiness with a sweet, heavy power that made her shudder with exquisite relief. He took her in his arms, heated skin against skin, the damp hair on his chest tingling against the soft crush of her breasts, his mouth finding and taking hers into another wild dimension of passion.

Her hands moved down his back, feeling the tension and clench of his muscles, exulting in his maleness, in the strength that complemented her softness. She moved languidly beneath him, intensifying the realisation of their physical intimacy.

He growled a deep animal sound as he lifted himself, taking his weight on his hands, answering her movement with a slow, voluptuous thrust of his hips that spiralled into deep penetration.

Her moan of ecstatic delight made his eyes gleam with a wild triumph, but she could see the strain of control in the tautness of his features. He was holding back for her, wanting to give her every intense nuance of pleasure, and Elizabeth was suddenly flooded with a feeling that went beyond anything physical.

'I want whatever you want,' she whispered, lifting herself to meet his need.

'I want you to want me as you've wanted no other man,' he breathed in harsh elation. 'Then I want you to want me as you never will want any other man. Then . . . and only then . . . will I be satisfied.'

His eyes seared hers with the primitive demand of his possession as he began a series of movements that played a tantalising and endlessly provocative rhythm, combining a fast savage taking and a slow, controlled languor that drove Elizabeth along a mounting tide of frenetic excitement. Sweat bathed their bodies. Their breath came faster. He spoke her name, said things that aroused her to a wilder response, and all constraint left him as they goaded each other towards the ultimate release of all sense of self.

'Now!' he cried.

And as she felt his body jerk deeply within her, her own responded with a convulsive melting, fusing, exulting in a blissful fulfilment that transcended her whole existence, and joined her to him for a moment in time that could never be taken away from her.

She wound her arms around him and held him tight to her heart, wanting the moment to stretch on and on into an eternity of togetherness, fiercely denying time and any other reality but this.

CHAPTER EIGHT

'COME to Noosa with me.'

The words broke the silence which had been like a protective cocoon to the lingering intimacy of their lovemaking. Elizabeth had hung on to it, afraid to let anything threaten the contentment which was so incredibly unique in her whole life's experience. She didn't want to talk or discuss anything, but knew she had to bow to the inevitable sooner or later. She wished it wasn't now. She wasn't ready yet—but then she probably never would be, and Price left her no choice.

He moved from her embrace, stretching out beside her, his head propped up on one arm so that he could look down at her. His eyes were warm. His mouth wore a soft curve of sensual satisfaction. His hand stroked the dark cloud of her hair away from her face.

'Come with me, Elizabeth. I have to go back tonight—I promised Ricky. But I can easily ring up and book you on a flight with me. We can spend the rest of the school vacation together. Relax in the sun, go boating on the estuary—do anything we fancy doing. There's nothing to keep you here, is there?'

It was too much for Elizabeth to take in straight away. She hadn't been thinking about the future. Her mind had been too busy soaking in and savouring the incredible present to do any thinking ahead. But the first thing that penetrated her reluctance to face up to the end of now was that Price did not want to leave her. He wanted her to go with him . . . be with him.

'Elizabeth?'

The quizzical note in his voice and the slight frown between his eyes denoted puzzlement at her lack of reaction. He bent down and kissed her, intent on arousing the response he wanted and, with relief surging through her, Elizabeth happily abandoned herself to the passionate sensuality of his demand.

'Say you'll come with me,' he breathed, still brushing her lips with his.

She opened her eyes and instantly fell victim to the blaze of command in his. 'Yes,' she whispered.

He smiled, his whole face lighting with pleasure and triumph. He looked so devastatingly handsome that Elizabeth's heart contracted. She reached up to stroke his cheek, hardly able to believe this was all happening to her—that it was real. He moved his head so that he could kiss her palm, and there was a soft gloating in his eyes as he watched her draw in a quick breath.

'Don't tell me ever again that you're no good at anything, Elizabeth,' he said emphatically. 'You're everything a man could ever want.'

She touched his lips in soft acknowledgement of his skill in lovemaking. 'It was you . . .'

'And you,' he insisted, biting playfully at her fingertips before grinning his contentment. 'We're good together. And to ensure more togetherness, I'll go and call the airline now.'

He rolled off the bed and reached for his clothes. Elizabeth watched him, still in a daze of wonderment. She no longer saw any threat in his aggressive masculinity. The long, lean power of his body was beautiful. She regretted it being covered by the trousers and shirt that Price hastily pulled on.

'How long will it take you to get ready?' he asked, his eyes smiling over her languid immobility. 'Not that there's any hurry. In fact, you can stay there just like that and I'll be right back. I'll book us on the last flight out.'

His departure from the bedroom prompted Elizabeth into thinking what she had to do to get ready. There were ten days left of the mid-year break—ten days of being with Price...

And Ricky!

Elizabeth sat bolt upright in bed, all her warm wonderful thoughts shattered by one small, but terribly significant, reality—a five-year-old child who could not be ignored or overlooked! A very special child to whom she owed a very special responsibility.

Elizabeth shot out of bed, snatched her dressing-gown from the wardrobe, and was still thrusting her arms into it as she ran out to the living-room. Price was already talking into the telephone receiver, enquiring about departure times. He raised his eyebrows at her as she made frantic gestures at him.

'Stop!' she cried in desperation. 'I can't go with you!'

His eyes sharpened in displeasure and Elizabeth felt sick with disappointment. But it was not in her nature to be blindly selfish at the cost of hurting anyone, let alone an innocent child.

Price said something about calling the airline back, then slowly replaced the receiver. The tawny-yellow eyes probed hers with urgent intensity. 'What's the problem, Elizabeth?' he asked quietly.

'Ricky!' she blurted out, hugging the gown around her. She began to shiver, more from reaction than the cold air.

Price frowned at her obvious agitation. 'Ricky will be delighted to have you with us.'

'Don't you see? That's the trouble!' Elizabeth cried, wishing there was some way around the problem, but already knowing it was impassable.

Price shook his head. 'I don't see. In fact, there's nothing I could do that would make Ricky happier than to——'

'Exactly!' Elizabeth broke in emphatically, her eyes deeply pained as she added, 'And what happens at the end of the vacation, Price? As it is, Ricky has a king-size pupil-teacher crush on me. If I go with you, he might start fantasising about me as a mother-figure. You said he misses not having a mother. And he'll be hurt when you . . . when I . . . when things don't work out the way he wants,' she finished dismally.

He stared at her as if she had slapped a brick in his face.

She gestured a helpless appeal. 'If it was just you and me . . . you must see the problem, Price! If I was unknown to Ricky it wouldn't matter so much. But . . .'

'But he'll talk at school, and your good reputation will be blown to the winds,' he drawled, a bitter mockery glinting in the tawny-yellow eyes, making them look hard and cruel. 'A lunch with me is something you can rationalise away, but any talk about our being lovers——'

'That's not the point!' Elizabeth snapped, too upset to temper her voice.

'Isn't it?' he taunted. 'Well, you tell me what you want, Elizabeth. A little hole-and-corner affair that serves to explore the sensuality you enjoyed today? As long as there's no risk of getting more involved than that, of course.'

The blood drained from her face as the beautiful accord they had shared slid into something sordid and nasty. She hadn't actually thought of what she wanted from what had developed between them. It had all happened too fast—unplanned and unexpected.

'You haven't said what you want with me, Price,' she replied defensively.

'Yes, I have,' he retorted, his eyes scorning any lack of comprehension on her part. 'I want the kind of open, honest relationship that would involve my son. But you've just made it clear that you won't even consider the possibility that it might work out right. You've already got us separated in your mind.'

'And what about the possibility that it works out wrong?' she flashed back at him, resenting his one-sided point of view. 'It won't affect your life. I just disappear out of it. But Ricky and I are left facing each other with memories day after day. You're asking too much too soon, Price.'

'Am I?' His mouth curled in derision. 'Will it make any difference if I ask in a week from now?

In a month? In a year? I'll still be Price Domenico. And Ricky will still be my son.'

He walked forward, his eyes glittering with a savagery that made her flinch when he paused beside her. 'Not even for you will I play the role of stud behind closed doors,' he grated, then touched her cheek in a mocking salute. 'But thank you for the illusion of something special while it lasted. If you'll excuse me, I'll finish dressing and get out of your life.'

He moved past her, into the bedroom. Elizabeth stood frozen to the spot, chilled to the bone by his words, and too confused to argue anything. But she was right. Had to be. The decision she was taking was the only responsible choice she had.

Price was twisting everything around the wrong way—reading false meanings into her concern, and giving her motives that hadn't entered her mind.

And what they had shared *had* been special! Not an illusion!

But it didn't follow that everything between them would be perfect. He might expect more than she was prepared to give... like her father... like Simon... and make her life miserable if she didn't give in to him. The way he was making her miserable now—condemning her for not falling in with his plan for their relationship. Condemning her for even questioning it!

Agitation shook her out of her frozen state and set her pacing the living-room, each step working up a righteous indignation. He didn't care about the difficulties in her teaching job. He didn't even think about the study she had to do or the examinations she wanted to pass. He probably considered her plans totally irrelevant, particularly if they interfered with the togetherness he wanted.

Elizabeth was in a fever of resentment by the time Price walked out of the bedroom. The moment she looked up and saw him—distant and formal in his dark grey suit—a terrible pain squeezed her heart. He was leaving her—leaving and never coming back. A cold, taut pride was stamped on his face, and the tawny-yellow eyes were strangely opaque, totally without expression as they skated over her one last time.

Elizabeth was wretchedly conscious of looking a complete mess—her body huddled in the shapeless woollen dressing-gown, her hair in wild disarray—but that didn't matter. She didn't want Price leaving like this. She had to stop him.

'You're not being fair!' she pleaded. 'You're . . . you're demanding a commitment with far-reaching consequences——'

'All commitments have consequences, Elizabeth,' he said curtly. 'You balance the possible gains against the possible losses and make your choice. I made my choice. You made yours. They don't match, and that's all there is to it.'

'But . . .' Her hands fluttered helplessly as she strove for another appeal. She felt as if she were swimming against an undertow that would inexorably drag her away from the goal she desperately needed to reach. 'We hardly know each other, Price. Can't we simply meet and——'

He made an impatient sound that cut off her fumbling attempt to appease. His eyes flashed contempt. 'How much do you need to know, Elizabeth? I've given you more of myself than I've given anyone in years. More than I care to remember right now.'

She flushed as she recalled the painful confidences he had shared with her. 'I meant...couldn't we be friends...for a while? We don't have to be lovers.'

'Don't we?' He shook his head, his mouth curling in derision of her argument. 'We've gone beyond that, Elizabeth. You know it. I know it. So let's part now while there's still no damage done.'

He walked to the door, opened it, and threw her a last crooked smile. 'Good luck with your exams.'

Then he was gone—gone before she could even call out his name.

CHAPTER NINE

THE beginning of the new school term was a blessing to Elizabeth. She needed to work, and work among people—children, teachers, parents—the more the better. Anything to distract her mind from the one person who had continually tormented it over the last ten days.

Her pleasure and satisfaction in being single and free was a past memory that she couldn't even summon any more. She felt more alone than she had ever felt in her life. And utterly miserable.

At night, when she lay awake in her bed, her body ached for the loving that Price had shown her. Even in sleep he haunted her dreams. But the days were the worst of all. Her thoughts whirled continually around the one tortured question—had she made the worst mistake of her life in denying the relationship that could have been?

It was unanswerable.

And it was futile.

The moment was gone—the decision made.

This was her life, Elizabeth insisted to herself as she swept her gaze around the classroom. She determinedly garnered the evidence of her effectiveness as a teacher: the artwork pinned to the walls, the results of the last class project proudly displayed on the cork-board, the shelves of carefully classified books to stimulate eager minds.

There was a knock on the door.

A parent, Elizabeth thought, pushing herself up from her desk. Or a grandparent, her mind added with relentless reasoning. The image of Mrs Wetherington-Jones's appalled face at the Regent sliced through Elizabeth's enforced composure.

But the door opened before she reached it, and a small head peered around it—a head with curly black hair, and sherry-brown eyes that raised a hopeful appeal to hers and wrung her heart.

'May I come in, miss?'

'Ricky, you know the rules,' she said sternly, struggling to contain the emotional turmoil he evoked. 'No children in the classroom before the first morning-bell.'

'But then the others will be here, and I've got something to give you,' he argued imploringly.

She hesitated, tempted not only by the gift, but her need to know if Ricky's father was somehow behind it—telling her something, holding out a link by which they could get back together if she was willing.

'Please? It'll only take a minute,' Ricky pushed, sensing an advantage and triumphantly snatching it.

In that moment he was so like his father that all sense of discipline was hopelessly lost. 'Just for a minute, then,' Elizabeth heard herself say, and Ricky was in with the door shut behind him before she could have second thoughts.

He lifted his school-bag on to the nearest desk and quickly zipped it open. He prattled on excitedly as he dug into the bag for the gift.

'Daddy and I went up to Noosa. That's on the Sunshine Coast in Queensland. And we had a great time, Miss Kent. We had a boat trip to Frazer Island to see the rain forest and all the bird-life. And we went fishing. You should have seen the fish I caught! And we spotted two koala bears in the National Forest on our walks...'

His arm whipped out of the bag, and in his hand was a tissue-wrapped object shaped like a large egg. '...but this is what I found on the beach. Daddy got some stuff so we could clean it out properly, because it smelled a bit. And I polished it all up. It's the best shell I've ever found,' he said proudly, and his eyes clung to hers, begging for love and approval as he offered it to her.

Tears pricked at Elizabeth's eyes as she unwrapped the gift. She could have been with them, sharing...

'It's a tiger cowrie, and it's not chipped or anything,' Ricky assured her.

As the tissue paper fell away to reveal the perfect shell, its tiger pattern and colours gleaming up at her, it became an insidious reminder of tawny-yellow and sherry-brown eyes.

'It's beautiful, Ricky. Thank you very much,' she said huskily.

'Daddy said you could use it as a paperweight for your notes. But if you lift it up to your ear, you can hear the sea.'

Somehow she found the presence of mind to lift it to her ear. She even managed a strained smile. 'So you can. Thanks again, Ricky. You'd better run along now and join the other children. Rules are rules,' she reminded him gently.

'Yes, Miss Kent,' he sighed, dutifully zipping his bag shut and carrying it back to the door. He paused with his hand on the knob and shot her one last soulful look. 'You will keep it, won't you?'

'Always,' she promised him.

The happiness that shone from his smile was Elizabeth's undoing. Fortunately the door closed between them before the welling tears overflowed and began trickling down her cheeks. She walked blindly back to her desk, sat down, rewrapped the shell, hid it at the back of a drawer, and buried her face in her hands.

Price had only been indulging his son. The suggestion that she might use the shell as a paper-weight for her notes was a clear indication that he was expecting her to get on with her life—without him. And as far as Ricky was concerned, nothing had changed since last term. It wasn't about to change for her, either.

Single . . . free . . . and childless!

All these years she had sublimated that innermost need with caring for the children she taught. But never had she felt the pain of deprivation as savagely as she did now.

Simon had put off the idea of having children. He had wanted to enjoy a big slice of life first, before getting tied down with the hassles of having a family. When he died as he did, leaving her with no support whatsoever and a lot of debts besides, Elizabeth had been grateful for Simon's refusal to accommodate her wishes. But if she could have had a child like Ricky . . .

She wished—however stupid it was—that it had been possible for her to fall pregnant that afternoon with Price. She hadn't even considered such a consequence at the time, despite the fact that she had long ago dismissed any need for contraceptive precautions. But as it happened, she had been completely safe. There was no chance of having Price Domenico's child.

If she had gone with him to Noosa...

But where would that have led? It wasn't as if he had asked her to marry him. And she wouldn't have said yes if he had. Not without resolving a lot of things first. And he had had no patience with her. She had to stop thinking about him. Had to...

The school-bell rang, and Elizabeth frantically mopped up her tears. She had made her choice, she told herself sternly, and there was nothing left to do but live by it. By the time her pupils filed into the classroom, she was ready and waiting for them, imbued by a determined sense of purpose.

The long days ploughed slowly into weeks. Elizabeth survived them in her own fashion—through stubborn grit and rigid self-discipline. She even found some joy in achieving the goals she set herself. One of her history essays earned the highest mark she had ever received, as well as a note of praise from the lecturer. And the two pupils in her class who were particularly precocious and troublesome finally settled into more productive attitudes.

Mrs Wetherington-Jones kept a frosty eagle eye on little Stephanie's progress. Although the woman never once mentioned Price Domenico's name, she made it very obvious that Elizabeth's breeding was now suspect—that she was not to be trusted as a person or as a teacher. Every time she poked her blue-blooded nose into the classroom, Elizabeth's tact and discretion were tested to the limit. But she managed to keep her claws sheathed.

She didn't manage quite so well when the Hartley trial began. Public interest in the case was high, and the daily newspapers fed it with sensational headlines. Once again it dominated the conversation in the staff-room at lunchtime. The man was prejudged as guilty. No one had a good word to say about him.

Elizabeth was the most junior member of the staff, and as such she had tended to listen respectfully to the older members' opinions rather than push her own. However, listening had led to her terrible misjudgement of Price Domenico, and the cynical bias over Hartley got to the point where Elizabeth could no longer sit on the fence and keep biting her tongue.

'The presumption of the law is that a person is innocent until proven guilty,' she burst out one day, startling everyone with her pent-up vehemence. In the silence that followed the statement, she held the floor and made the most of it.

'I happen to think Hartley was doing a great job. He was cleaning up the police force. He set up that security system to stop vandalism in public schools. He tightened up the prison sentences on those offenders who were a menace to society. Particularly drug-pushers. Now why would he do that if he was taking bribes to cover up drug-dealing? It seems more logical to me that some people would want him out of the way because he *wasn't* corrupt. That's why I think the man is innocent.'

She swept all the staff-members with a scathing look. 'Everyone forgets the good things a person has done when a juicy bit of dirt gets smeared around. If that's human nature, then thank heaven for the law. There is a chance that Hartley will be found innocent.'

'That's the most stupid thing I've ever heard,' drawled one of the older teachers. 'There is no one in this world who cannot be bent, if the price is right. Besides which, if you read the newspaper reports, you'll know that the prosecution is steadily driving the nails into Hartley's coffin.'

'The defence hasn't started yet,' Elizabeth shot back at him, riled by his condescending and insulting comment.

'And who has he got defending him?' came the derisive taunt. 'None other than Price Domenico. And we all know what that means.'

'I don't think we all know what that means at all!' Elizabeth returned hotly, suffering a severe rush of blood to the head. She eyed them all fiercely. 'Have any of you met Price Domenico?'

No one answered.

'Well, I have!' Elizabeth said triumphantly. 'And he's as straight as you can get. Not only on the right side of the law, but dedicated to the spirit of justice. Which is more than you can say about the spirit behind this conversation. In fact, none of the things you say about Price Domenico are true, and I'm sick to death of hearing them.'

'What about old Joe Domenico?'

The sceptical snort fired Elizabeth further.

'He catered for people who like to throw away their money gambling. And he gave away more of it than a lot of our so-called upstanding citizens ever do. He was a generous——'

'She's got Ricky Domenico in her class,' someone interrupted, apparently an indulgent excuse for Elizabeth's uncharacteristic outburst.

'Yes, I have,' Elizabeth stormed on. She had the bit between the teeth now, and would not back away for anything. 'He's a good kid who deserves a fair go. And I don't see how he's going to get that if the staff of this school persists in bad-mouthing his father and his grandfather. It's not right. No more right than saying someone is guilty until he is proven innocent. As far as I can see, everyone in this room who persists with that attitude has the world upside-down!'

An awkward silence ensued. No one moved a muscle. Then the staff cynic drawled, 'Well, Elizabeth . . . when Hartley is proven innocent, you can have the pleasure of telling us all you told us so.'

General laughter effectively ended the conversation. It was more embarrassed than mocking, and Elizabeth felt satisfied that she had made a few telling points. In the days that followed she was subjected to a bit of snide ribbing about the Hartley case, but no one said anything derogatory about Price Domenico or his father. At least, not within her hearing. And that made Elizabeth feel that she had paid some of her debt to Price. Although the thousand dollars he had returned still didn't sit well on her conscience, despite his reasoning.

Ironically enough, Elizabeth wasn't quite sure that Price would appreciate her championing his cause. She recalled how caustic he had been on that particular matter. Nevertheless, she felt better about having made a stand for justice and right, and Price didn't know about it, anyway.

He wouldn't ever know what she said or thought or did any more—except through Ricky—and the pain of loss she felt was way out of proportion with the short time she had spent with him.

A week passed. The prosecution rested its case in the Hartley trial, and the defence began. Suddenly there were new names being dragged before the public, names that raised eyebrows and put an entirely different complexion on the case—and one name in particular that belonged to a politician who was a dear friend of Mrs Wetherington-Jones.

Which gave Elizabeth quite a lot of secret satisfaction—until the headmaster requested a meeting with her after school-hours and she learnt the depth of spite in the woman. Elizabeth was asked to bring all Richard Domenico's school records to the meeting, but not even that unusual request prepared her for what Mr Fairchild had to say.

The headmaster was not in fine form this afternoon. His greeting was brief—almost curt—and he asked Elizabeth to help herself to the afternoon tea which was set on a tray at one side of his massive desk. He did not chat. He studied Ricky's records and, although no five-year-old pupil could have had better, they obviously gave the headmaster no pleasure. He was scowling as he closed the folder Elizabeth had presented to him.

'Is there a problem about Ricky?' Elizabeth asked, unable to contain her concern any longer.

Mr Fairchild sagged back in his throne-like chair, his authoritative aura definitely dimmed. He looked tired, strained, and thoroughly fed up with whatever was exercising his mind. His sharp blue eyes stabbed at Elizabeth with anger and resentment, yet she sensed that those feelings were not really directed at her.

'Tomorrow afternoon there is to be a meeting of the school-board. There has been a considerable amount of politicking going on this last week, to the effect that one item on the agenda is the suitability of Richard Domenico's remaining as a pupil at Alpha Academy. So, yes—there is a problem.'

Elizabeth was so shocked that she could barely gather her wits. 'But . . . he's done nothing wrong. He . . . he can't be expelled without any reason.'

Mr Fairchild heaved a weary sigh. 'This is a private establishment, Miss Kent. The board has the authority to expel any pupil it wants to. It is under no compulsion to state a reason. And if it does, it can give a reason so general that it cannot be challenged. In this case, I consider such a move highly dangerous. The reputation of Alpha Academy could be severely damaged. This is politics at work, and politics at its dirtiest and nastiest!'

He made a savage grimace. 'I argued for Richard Domenico to be accepted. And I shall argue against his expulsion. But there are forces at work which may override the weight of my opinion. There is nothing I can do if I'm outvoted. Except resign in protest. That is how far this matter is going.'

Elizabeth heard the words and didn't believe them. 'The good of the school . . .' she prompted.

'Yes . . .' He lifted his hands to gesture his painful dilemma. 'Resignation might be going too far. After all, it is only one child. But it's not good, Miss Kent. Not good for my authority. My judgement being challenged . . .' He corrected his expression to lofty purpose. 'And it's a matter of principle!'

'It's Mrs Wetherington-Jones, isn't it?' Elizabeth bit out furiously, too outraged to play polite games. 'She's the trouble-maker!'

'Mrs Wetherington-Jones is but one member of the board,' came the automatic reproof. But the headmaster did not look affronted by her conclusion or her uncontrolled manner. In fact, he was viewing Elizabeth with a wary weighing look, as if he wanted to add something but wasn't sure if it was wise.

'Isn't there anything we can do to stop this bigotry?' she cried in angry protest.

'There is nothing that either you or I can do, Miss Kent. If the board remains obdurate in their present intention,' he said very slowly, 'then that will be that! However, there is one more day before the meeting. Perhaps their minds can be changed. Pressures can be overturned by other pressures. This is a power-game, Miss Kent, where people are playing for their egos and their reputations. But, as you are already starting to learn, I will not be beaten until the final vote is taken.'

Elizabeth sensed he was leading up to something important, but she couldn't guess what it was. She kept silent, waiting, every nerve tensed in urgent anticipation for some answer that would help Ricky.

The headmaster leaned forward, rested his forearms on the desk, linked his hands, and peered sharply at her under lowered eyebrows. 'I have been given to understand that you know Richard Domenico's father personally, Miss Kent.'

Elizabeth vividly recalled her outburst in the staff-room, and a self-conscious flush burnt into her cheeks. 'I have met Mr Domenico and talked to him. He defended me against a charge of negligent driving and proved I was innocent,' she stated earnestly, not knowing if she was about to be criticised for the association, but determined to uphold her right to associate with whoever she liked. Outside school-time.

The headmaster didn't blink an eye. He continued to regard her steadily, if a little uneasily. 'It was reported to me that you and Price Domenico lunched together at the Regent Hotel.'

Mrs Wetherington-Jones at work again! Elizabeth seethed. Her chin came up defiantly. 'That's true. We did. It was on the day of the court-case, and I was very grateful for all the trouble he'd gone to on my behalf.'

The headmaster frowned and looked down at his hands. He worked his fingers together for several moments before he spoke again, his gaze still lowered as if concerned about embarrassing her.

'It occurred to me that you might have been seeing Richard's father on a more personal basis. And, I hasten to add, that is your private business, Miss Kent. I would not normally intrude on such matters. Providing they have no relevance to the smooth running of Alpha Academy. But if you were friendly with him . . .' He paused and shot her a hard, meaningful look. '. . . Price Domenico is the kind of man who can look after his own.'

Elizabeth needed no further prompting to absorb the point. Her heart leapt in agitation at the thought of going to him, seeing him, but of course she had to. It was perfectly clear that the headmaster thought Price was the only person who had a chance of turning the tide of opinion on the school-board. If Ricky was not to have the black mark of expulsion against his name, she had to act, and act fast!

It was also perfectly clear that Mr Fairchild was carefully distancing himself from any direct hand in the manoeuvre.

Power-games!

And if the dispute came to a crunch, she was the scapegoat who had let the cat out of the bag—a junior teacher who was easily replaceable. But that didn't matter. She hadn't planned to stay on at Alpha Academy once she got her university degree. It was the injustice to Ricky that had to be stopped at all costs. Whether Price could stop it was another question, but at least she could give him fair warning.

She had to see him for that purpose—if no other. But the gnawing hunger inside her fed on the opportunity to find out if there was still a chance to change the course of her life—a chance with him.

Elizabeth wasn't aware of the eager light spilling through the anxiety that shadowed her eyes. But the headmaster took considerable satisfaction from it. He smiled and slid smoothly on to his next tack.

'I've been very impressed with your work, Miss Kent. A dedicated, caring teacher—just the type we want here at Alpha Academy. When your contract with us comes up for renewal at the end of the year, I will have no hesitation in recommending that you be retained on the staff.'

The bribe, Elizabeth thought cynically. 'It's kind of you to say so, Mr Fairchild. Thank you,' she said. She wanted to ask him if he was prepared to put it in writing. But an inner voice whispered that there was no way he would commit himself that far. As Price had said, in this pragmatic world justice was all too often a bad joke.

The headmaster pushed himself up from his desk, once more cloaking himself in benevolent authority. 'I won't keep you any longer, Miss Kent. Thank you for your time.' He tapped his finger on Ricky's folder. 'We can only hope that the board will see reason. These records prove that Richard Domenico is an asset to Alpha Academy.'

Elizabeth made all the correct responses to his smooth patter as he ushered her out of his office. There was nothing more of any import to be said. She knew what was expected of her, and he knew that she knew. And she would do it. But not to save Mr Fairchild's face—nor for the greater good of Alpha Academy!

CHAPTER TEN

A HIGH brick security wall fronted the street. Large double-gates in strong iron lacework obviously led to garages. A smaller, but no less formidable gate apparently opened to a path which led to the house. Lighted windows indicated that someone was home. Elizabeth hoped that it was Price.

She paid the driver and alighted from the taxi. It was eight o'clock. If Ricky followed the normal routine of a five-year-old, he should be in bed. As fond as she was of the little boy, Elizabeth didn't want him complicating this meeting with Price. It was going to be difficult enough as it was. She prayed that her timing was right, that Price was home, had already dined, and they could talk together... alone!

She had no idea how many people comprised Price's household, but she imagined there would have to be a live-in housekeeper to look after his son and run his home. It was a big house, not quite a mansion, but double-storeyed and set on a large block of land, as were many of the older homes in Hunter's Hill—the fashionable homes that had tennis-courts and swimming-pools and views of Sydney Harbour.

Elizabeth's heart hammered nervously as she pushed open the small gate and closed it behind her. It was a long path to the house, and the lawns and flourishing garden-beds suggested that someone was employed to look after them. She had gone only a few yards when lights were turned on, flooding the pathway.

Elizabeth's pulse leapt in agitation. She paused in her step, wondering if she had triggered some alarm. The front door opened and a burly red-haired man stepped out on to the veranda. He closed the door behind him and stood waiting for her approach.

Elizabeth forced herself forwards. The closer she got to him, the more ugly and formidable the man looked. He had the shoulders of an ox, and his face had the mashed appearance of a fighter who had spent too many years in the ring. Yet when he spoke, his voice was friendly and pleasant.

'Your name and business, please, ma'am?'

She took a deep breath to calm her jumpy nerves. 'I'm Elizabeth Kent, and I...'

'Ricky's teacher!' A broad grin split his face and a hammy hand was thrust out to her. 'Well, you sure are a pretty one. Pleased to meet you, Miss Kent. I'm Les Briggs. I look after Ricky.'

'You?' Elizabeth croaked weakly as her slender hand received a bone-crushing shake.

'Sure! Drive him to and from school, keep him happy with things. I do the garden, too.' His eyes sparkled. 'Bet you got a surprise when the lights came on.'

'Yes. I did,' Elizabeth choked out, startled by the guileless simplicity in the man.

'Ricky and I fixed up this electronic beam across the path. Puts the lights on, so visitors won't trip over themselves in the dark. We have a lot of fun together, me and Ricky. He's a swell kid, isn't he?'

'Yes,' Elizabeth agreed, recovering her wits with some difficulty.

The security wall, the triggered lights, the look of the man—for a few moments she had been thrown right off balance, the spectre of Joe Domenico's underworld clouding her mind. But of course, it had to be wrong. That was a thing of the past. And while Les Briggs might not have the most prepossessing countenance, the mind and heart behind his battered face had the innocence of a child.

'Is Mr Domenico home, Mr Briggs?' she asked with more confident aplomb.

'Come right on in, Miss Kent,' he said, re-opening the front door wide in invitation. 'Price won't say no to seeing you,' he added with a chuckle, then threw her an encouraging wink. 'He's had his nose to the grindstone with this court-case. I reckon, though, that if anyone can remind him there are some nicer things in life, it'll be you, Miss Kent.'

Elizabeth wasn't quite sure how to respond to the heavy-handed compliment. But she was not about to argue the point. She had to see Price Domenico.

Les Briggs led her down a wide hallway to a set of double-doors which were directly opposite the foot of a wide cedar staircase. He gave a brief knock on one of the doors, opened it, poked his head into the room and casually announced, 'Visitor for you, Price.' Then, with a grin on his face that would have done a Cheshire cat proud, he stood back and waved Elizabeth inside.

It wasn't easy taking those last few steps, not knowing what kind of reception waited for her. They drained all of Elizabeth's courage. She was shaking inside as the door closed behind her, leaving her alone with the man who had chosen to walk out of her life as abruptly as he had entered it.

Price was sprawled along one of three long chesterfields which were grouped around an open fire. Papers were strewn over a central coffee-table. He was holding a many-paged document that he had obviously been reading. He looked much the same as he had when she had first seen him: coatless, tieless, his shirt-sleeves rolled up his forearms, black curls flopping on to his forehead.

For several moments it was as if he were caught in a freeze-frame, disbelief stamped on his face. Then a wary reserve flicked any openness from his expression. He swung his long legs off the cushions, and slowly pushed himself to his feet.

He offered no greeting. Elizabeth herself was incapable of speech, totally tongue-tied by the sheer magnetism of his presence. He stared at her, and Elizabeth fiercely willed him to feel the same attraction.

She had deliberately worn her hair loose, the thick, wavy mass of it held away from her face by a side-comb over each ear. The dark red dress hugged her figure, emphasising its femininity, while its simplicity of style lent it a quiet elegance. She felt her skin heat and prickle with excitement as the tawny-yellow gaze noted every detail of her appearance with a slow thoroughness that tautened every nerve in her body.

But the tension wasn't wholly hers. Although Price stood completely still, she could sense the tightly coiled expectancy that he kept rigidly clamped. She suddenly realised that he was waiting for her to speak, to tell him the reason for her visit. She did her best to work some moisture into her dry mouth. Her eyes clung to his, desperately searching, pleading for a ready acceptance of the offer she had come to make.

'I...I hope I'm not interrupting important work,' she said weakly. He still held the document in his hands. It was almost certainly something to do with the Hartley case.

'Nothing that can't wait,' he said tautly, his gaze locked on to hers, compelling her to say more.

She couldn't start with the school problem. She knew intuitively that this was the moment to reach out to Price—and if she prevaricated the moment might be forever lost behind other issues. It had to be now. And yet, even though her overwhelming need for him demanded instant and open expression, fear choked the words in her throat. If he answered with cynicism, with scorn...

'Well, Elizabeth?' he prompted, but the words held a rough thickness that suggested he was fighting emotional conflict, too.

'I was wrong not to go to Noosa with you,' she blurted out, terrified of rejection, but forcing herself to bare her heart and mind, no matter how vulnerable it made her feel. This was her one and only chance to retrieve the mistake she had made.

Something flickered through the guarded eyes, a burning gleam that was swiftly dampened. 'I'm sorry I forced you...beyond what you deemed right for yourself... and for Ricky,' he said stiffly. 'At the time, I'd forgotten your desire to remain free... and single.'

'I was wrong about that, too,' she answered wildly.

The fabric of his shirt stretched tight across his chest as he drew in a deep breath. Conflicting emotions worked across his face, and the tawny-yellow eyes glittered into dangerous life. 'Elizabeth... are you saying what I think you're saying?' he asked tautly.

Her voice trembled with the enormity of the questions she had to put to him, but she pushed the words out. 'Would you ask me again, Price? Do you still want me?'

The document fell from his hand and pages went scattering. Elizabeth's feet found that they could move after all, and she met him half-way across the room, sinking gratefully into his warmth and strength as he caught her against him with arms that wound around her like hoops of steel.

He groaned, his cheek rubbing over her hair in an agony of yearning. 'You don't know how many times I nearly... but that doesn't matter now. You're here...'

His hands were hard, roughly possessive as they crushed her softness against him in his need to affirm her reality, and the long-frustrated hunger in him stirred an immediate desire that left Elizabeth in no doubt as to his wanting her. The quivery excitement of her own response was just as swift.

'Price...' It was half a plea, half a protest, fused by the uncontrollable strength of the feelings he aroused.

'I know,' he sighed, his voice furred with reluctance. 'I know what this has cost you. I know the pain you must have felt. But this time we will get it right between us. As best we can.'

A light shudder ran through him as he exerted the control to pull away from her. His hands lifted to cup her face, tenderly stroking the softness of her skin. His eyes were liquid gold, vibrant with barely suppressed emotion.

'Elizabeth . . . I know you're afraid to let me into your life . . . that if you give me the space I'll turn into some kind of tyrant. But I swear to you, I don't need to inflict that type of domination on a woman to prove myself a man. Or anything else. You're a very special person . . .'

'You are to me, too, Price,' she answered huskily. 'And I'm not asking for promises or guarantees. I thought . . . if you want to . . . we could try living together. But if that's presuming too much . . .'

'No!' He dragged in another deep breath and smiled at her with dazzling relief. 'No, that's not presuming too much.' He plucked the combs from her hair and ran his fingers back through the long tresses. 'To have you beside me is a dream I've been fighting every night.'

A terrible uncertainty flitted through her mind. 'Only in bed, Price?'

He laughed, a bubbling exultant laughter that confused Elizabeth until he answered her. 'Every night. But with you, every day, too. Beside me here . . . there . . . everywhere.' His hands dropped to hers. 'Come and sit down. I'll show you I mean it.'

He drew her to one of the chesterfields, sat her down, then skirted the coffee-table and sank on to the one opposite her. 'Take your shoes off. Curl up if you like. Be comfortable with me,' he instructed. His obvious pleasure in simply having her under his eyes warmed her soul.

Elizabeth smiled her own happy relief. She could not completely banish her apprehension that their relationship might not work out as easily as the resolution of it. Almost all her experience of life told her that this was a terrible gamble, with the odds heavily weighed towards her getting badly hurt. But she felt right about being here now.

'We still don't know each other very well,' she said ruefully, although the contented feeling that rippled through her body as she looked at him made a mockery of her words. Something inside her responded so positively to this man that it was almost as if he had always been part of her life—like part of a jigsaw that had been missing, but was now being slotted into place.

'Why did you come tonight, Elizabeth?' he asked, his eyes probing softly, wanting to understand her feelings.

She searched for the right words, knowing she had to give him complete honesty. 'Everything just seemed to come to a head this afternoon, Price. There's trouble at school. About Ricky.'

He frowned. 'What trouble?'

'The headmaster asked me for Ricky's class records. There's a meeting of the school-board tomorrow afternoon. I think Mrs Wetherington-Jones is behind it all, but whoever—whatever—the nub is that there's agitation for Ricky to be removed from the school. Mr Fairchild intends to fight it, but——'

Sheer savagery swept across Price's face. In an instant he was up, prowling the room, his whole body emanating a taut black fury. Any further word Elizabeth might have said choked in her throat. Every instinct in her body prickled with the sense of danger. She sat very still.

'They will not get to me through my son!' Price seethed, the tiger eyes slashing ruthless purpose at Elizabeth. 'They will not hurt my son because of me!'

His eyes narrowed and his lips curled into a vicious sneer. He made a harsh sound of contempt. 'All these years of looking askance at me—the slurs on the Domenico name—and I wouldn't have even bothered to use their kind of dirt. Immaterial. But I'll use it now.'

His voice dropped to a low threatening purr. 'No one . . . no one attacks my son and gets away unscathed.'

Elizabeth shivered. The violence of feeling that had vibrated from him on the morning of her court-case was a pale echo of what she sensed in him now. Then it had only been his integrity under attack. His child was a strike at his heart. As he stalked up and down the room, he looked even more lethal than any tiger with its cub endangered.

He swung around to face her, and suddenly stiffened to an abrupt halt. His expression changed, a turbulent conflict of dark emotions slowly fusing into a mask of bitter pride.

'So this is what brought you to me? This is the catalyst that changed your mind? Did Ricky's threatened expulsion make it easier for you, Elizabeth?'

His voice was hard, stinging with implications that Elizabeth didn't understand. She frowned, puzzled and frightened by the shift in his mood towards her. 'I thought you would want to know, Price. In case there was something you could do——'

'In case?' His eyes glittered at her as his mouth curled around the words, obviously not finding them to his taste. 'Did you find it less of a risk to invite a live-in relationship with me if Ricky wasn't to be your pupil any more? No innocent child around to blurt out that you were cohabiting with Price Domenico? Was it that factor which made up your mind about us, Elizabeth?'

'No!' She shook her head vehemently as the import of his questions hit her. 'How can you even think that?' she cried in horror. 'I don't want Ricky expelled. I'd do anything to stop it. It's so terribly wrong and unjust. Surely you can see that it's against everything I believe in? It's the kind of thing that brought me to you in the first place!'

His chest rose and fell as he battled with whatever demons were driving him. 'So why give in tonight? Why offer yourself to me now? What's it supposed to be... a gesture of support in the face of injustice? Some *stupid* sense of debt you think you owe me?'

All colour whipped from Elizabeth's face. As shock gave way to stabbing pain, she pushed herself clumsily to her feet. She should have known he was no different from other men. The caring was only a façade to get what he wanted from her. And she would never measure up to anything much in his eyes. Never be given her due respect for the person she was.

'At least . . . I warned you,' she said, instinctively dragging on the shreds of what little dignity she had left. 'And I do feel . . . what I feel. It's not just because of Ricky.'

She turned and started towards the door, her legs heavy and listless, her head swimming with the effort required to dismiss what she had so desperately wanted.

'No!' He moved with lethal swiftness, blocking her path. He grabbed her upper arms, his fingers digging into her flesh with bruising domination. 'You're not going to run away, Elizabeth!' he commanded, his eyes burning into hers with a violence of feeling that ignited just as violent a rebellion against him.

'Get your hands off me!' she cried, her voice shaking with furious resentment. 'I will not . . . I will never submit to force again, Price Domenico. Not from any man!'

He looked distractedly at his hands, as if he hadn't realised what he'd done with them. 'I'm sorry,' he rasped, and instantly released her. His gaze flashed back to hers, no less compelling in spite of her protest. 'But I want answers, and I want the truth.'

'The truth is that you don't need anyone!' Elizabeth retorted fiercely. 'You don't want anyone standing up for you, or taking your side, even if it's done simply in the interests of fairness or decency. Never mind that it hurts me to hear others speak badly of you and your family. That it hurts me to see you and Ricky hurt. I'm supposed to stay silent and not lift a finger. Well, rest assured I'll keep right out of your affairs in future. You can do it all your own way!'

His mouth twisted. 'I am grateful to you. I wish circumstances were different—that you didn't have to feel that. But I certainly don't need you to martyr yourself in my cause. If you decided to live openly with me as some kind of protest or crusade——'

'Don't worry! You've just changed my mind. I don't need you, either. In fact, the last thing I need is to live with a man who thinks I'm stupid!' Despite the pain that was twisting through her, she drew up her shoulders, stiffened her spine, and lifted her head high 'If you'll kindly excuse me, I'll get out of your life. And stay out of it completely this time. I was a fool to come to you.'

He shook his head as though he were punch-drunk. 'Stop reacting! For heaven's sake, Elizabeth! I don't think you're stupid. Misguided, perhaps...'

'You said it!' she fired at him, her eyes flashing their hurt. 'You said I was stupid.'

The colour drained from his face and he stared at her in pained recollection of his own words. 'I didn't mean it that way, Elizabeth,' he said earnestly. 'I guess...I wanted you to come to me...free of all this. I wanted simply to be wanted. Because you wanted us to be together... for the good things we can share... but not the bad.' His eyes searched hers in a desperate, agonised plea. 'Can you understand that?'

She dropped her gaze as tears filmed her eyes. 'It's not going to work, Price,' she choked out. 'I thought being together meant sharing everything...the good and the bad. And you...you...'

She couldn't go on. The lump in her throat was impossible to circumvent without sobbing. Her shoulders sagged in defeat. But before she could bring herself to step away from Price, she found herself enfolded in his arms, the warmth and strength of his body seeping into hers, her head pressed gently on to his shoulder, his cheek rubbing softly over her hair.

'Forgive me,' he murmured, his voice deep and impassioned. 'I'm the stupid one, Elizabeth, not you. I've been alone too long. I'm not used to having anyone stand shoulder to shoulder with me...and I'm a fool to quench your fire and courage. It's what I admire most in you.'

He sighed. 'I feel that I should be protecting you, but that diminishes what you are, doesn't it? You were well-named after a string of queens, Elizabeth. A proud, indomitable spirit, and a caring heart.'

A quiver of pleasure took the edge off her pain. Never had anyone thought her worthy of the names she had been given. Her father had used them as a weapon of disapproval. Her husband had considered them a joke. But Price thought they suited her.

He stroked her hair with caring tenderness and, right or wrong, Elizabeth felt no inclination to move. After all, she was no longer quite so sure he thought her stupid. He was being very convincing the other way. And admitting he was in the wrong—not many men were as big as that. It reminded her just how special Price was. And she desperately wanted it to work out right.

'Please...' he murmured persuasively, his mouth sweeping warmly, tinglingly over her ear. 'Give me another chance, Elizabeth. I promise you—I'll work at our relationship. Be patient with me. I'll listen to you. I want to listen to you, hear all your thoughts, know all of you...'

She lifted her head back, vaguely seeking reassurance in his eyes. But any such intention was totally waylaid. His mouth covered hers with a seductive power that swamped her mind with the needs that only he had ever aroused in her. Every instinct, every nerve, every pulse of her blood surged to answer his, to reach the unison she had known with him—known and remembered every night without him.

'Elizabeth...' he whispered against her lips, and it was a plea, a demand, a hungry want that could not bear to go unanswered. 'Come with me... be with me... stay with me forever...'

He swept her along with him, and they were halfway up the staircase before Elizabeth even began to doubt or question the sense of where he led her. Her step faltered. She pulled back. Her eyes widened in fearful uncertainty. 'Price...'

'Hush,' he soothed. 'You'll waken Ricky.' And his eyes compelled her acquiescence as he softly added, 'Trust me.'

Elizabeth didn't know if she trusted him or not, but she went with him, drawn by the promise of what could be... and what would be. She didn't want to deny him. Her own need was too overwhelming. Blindly, recklessly, wantonly, she put off thinking—until afterwards.

He whirled her into a room and shut the door behind them, catching her to him with an urgency that sent wild shivers of response through her entire body. His mouth came down on hers, moving persuasively, tormentingly, until her arms wound around his neck and her lips parted, inciting a deeper, more erotic contact. She moaned soft and low in her throat as he took her invitation, and the aroused thrust of movement from his hips heightened the wild sensuality of his kiss. She arched eagerly against him, a melting warmth flooding her body. His hand moved up over her dress to cup her breast, stroking it, holding the swelling fullness of it, intoxicating her with more and more excitement.

'Not in the darkness,' he murmured, his lips grazing softly over her face. 'Not like a dream. I want to see you, Elizabeth.'

He held her hard against him as he bent to one side. A low lamplight flicked on, casting a soft glow around them. He touched her face, her throat, his hand slipping slowly around to the nape of her neck, finding the tag of her zip, drawing it down the curve of her back as he drew once more on the sweetness of her mouth with drugging sensuality.

The dress fell in a pool at her feet, her bra was deftly removed, and he pulled back from her and looked with aching desire at the soft, pale fullness of her breasts, their points hardening as he reached out and softly caressed them.

'I want to see you, too,' Elizabeth said huskily, lifting her own hands to the opening of his shirt.

He shuddered as her fingers flicked down the buttons, grazing the firm flesh beneath. She pushed the fabric from his shoulders, and the tips of her breasts brushed against his chest.

With a hoarse cry he tore off the shirt and crushed her against him, raining kisses over her face, down her throat, across her shoulders. His hands raked down her back, pushed at her remaining undergarments, seeking the intimate contact of flesh against flesh. He swung her on to the bed and stripped away the last offending clothes, and Elizabeth eagerly reached for him as he lowered the strong male weight of him over her quivering body.

She was aching in sweet anticipation for the intimate caresses he had bestowed on her before, and she longed to give him the same depth of pleasure. The desire that flooded through her obliterated all inhibitions, and she touched him tremulously, delicately, her eyes pleading more direction from him. He gasped. His eyes darkened. He kissed her with violent passion. And the surge of his taut manhood thrilled her beyond any thought of herself. She didn't want to wait. She wanted him inside her—to possess him and be possessed.

'Now...quickly,' she gasped, clutching him tightly as he moved his lips from hers.

'Elizabeth...' It was a groan of need and want that echoed deeply inside her.

'Yes...yes!' she urged wildly.

He lifted her, and for a moment he stayed poised against her, hesitating. She writhed in desperate welcome, inciting his entry with an instinctive, irresistible voluptuousness. She saw his chest heave, then, with a hoarse, driven cry, he plunged hard to the centre of her being, and the exquisite tension of waiting turned into a flooding tide of ecstatic release. He was there—in her, with her, part of her—and tears of sheer happiness welled into her eyes.

She heard him call her name—a ragged sound of both delight and despair—and he moved with uncontrolled wildness, with almost savage ferocity, building another tide of ever-mounting sensation with each pounding thrust of his possession. Then, like a star exploding within her, he took her with him into a blissful darkness where only she and he existed, fused as one for all eternity.

There was a sense of losing consciousness, a floating, cradled in warmth, and she gradually became aware of her name being murmured over and over again, with wonder and a sweet incredulous joy.

'Price,' she whispered, and it had the same sound to it. She breathed a soft sigh of contentment and snuggled closer to him. It was so good to have his warm nakedness next to her, to feel his arms around her, to know with absolute security that she was not alone.

Why everything was so incredibly different with him she didn't know, didn't care. He was beautiful, caring, loving, fierce and tender and utterly perfect. He gently stroked her hair, ran featherlight caresses over her back, and, like a kitten who had finally and gratefully found the best place of rest, Elizabeth drifted into a peaceful sleep, all the tension of decision dispelled by a fulfilment too deep to question.

She barely stirred when Price resettled her between the sheets of his bed and wrapped the warm eiderdown around her. Instinctively she nestled back against his body, and, although the temptation to caress her into sensitised wakefulness was strong, Price contented himself with the delight of holding her soft womanliness against him.

He had much to think about. To plan. It was only after he had worked out every detail of approach and attack—and the most desirable shape of the future that was now possible—that he allowed himself to completely relax and sink into sleep with the woman who lay shoulder to shoulder with him, side by side—where he would always keep her...if he won what he wanted.

CHAPTER ELEVEN

THE light stroke of fingertips on her cheek woke Elizabeth. The unfamiliarity of being touched was so startling that she snapped her eyelids open. A frisson of shock ran through her as her eyes met other eyes—as large as saucers and sherry-brown, fixed inexorably on her with a thousand question marks.

'I thought you might not be real,' the little boy whispered, awed by the reality in front of him. 'I didn't mean to wake you.'

It was light. It was morning. And the warm nakedness of Price Domenico's body behind her was a forceful reminder of her own nakedness and what she had done. What they had done! For a moment, sheer panic coursed through Elizabeth's veins. To be discovered like this! Without warning... without introduction... without any easing into the situation at all!

But she couldn't allow herself to panic. Ricky was staring at her, his cheeks slightly flushed, his eyes large and luminous with... was it hope? Certainly some inner excitement was shining through.

'It's all right, Ricky,' she whispered back, her hand frantically stroking down Price's powerfully muscled thigh, needing his help, his support. 'What time is it?' she asked the boy softly, keeping his attention fixed on her while she surreptitiously tried to wake his father.

'Six o'clock,' Ricky answered gravely. 'Daddy always lets me wake him up at six o'clock.' He took a deep breath, and it was clear he wanted to ask a question, but didn't quite dare.

'You must be surprised to see me here,' Elizabeth said gently, her fingernails digging into Price's firm flesh. He hadn't even stirred at her touch. Why didn't he wake up?

'Yes,' Ricky breathed. His eyes darted to the pillow where his father's face was buried in the long tangled tresses of Elizabeth's hair. 'Have you been here all night?' he asked ingenuously.

'Yes. I came to see your father after you'd gone to bed. He asked me to stay,' Elizabeth explained. 'I hope you don't mind.'

Ricky bit his lower lip and shook his head quite vehemently. His eyes clung to hers, obviously begging her to say more.

Elizabeth felt her way cautiously, hoping she was choosing the right words. 'I know I'm not your mother, Ricky, but your father said you would like to have me living here with both of you. Is that true? Or would you rather just have me as your teacher at school?'

The sherry-brown eyes lit up like fairy lights on a Christmas tree. 'You could be like a mother. There wouldn't be anyone I'd like better,' he breathed ecstatically. Then another thought struck him and he frowned anxiously. 'Would I have to keep calling you Miss Kent?'

'Not at home,' Elizabeth assured him, gathering confidence from his response. 'But I think at school...the other pupils wouldn't think it fair if you called me something different from them. So we'd better stick to Miss Kent there. When we're away from school, you could call me Elizabeth if you like. That's what your father calls me.'

Ricky heaved a delighted sigh. 'Elizabeth,' he said slowly, as if trying it out, then grinned at her in happy triumph.

She smiled back, relieved that he seemed to be accepting it all so easily, but felt another stab of anxiety when his face puckered up in a querulous fashion.

'Are you going to sleep with my daddy every night?'

Elizabeth's heart gave an agitated leap, and she took a deep breath to calm herself. 'Does that worry you, Ricky?' she asked him straight, wondering what on earth she would do if it did.

He gave her a down-and-up look that was full of hungry appeal. 'Could you sleep with me sometimes? Like a mother?'

His need twisted her heart. She hastily arranged the top sheet to keep her nakedness firmly covered, and lifted the eiderdown in welcoming invitation. 'Come and snuggle up, Ricky,' she smiled.

He dived into bed with her, giggling with excitement as she cuddled him close and dropped a kiss on his forehead. 'This is what mothers do,' she assured him. 'They don't sleep with their children, Ricky, but sometimes when children have bad dreams, or don't feel well, or just for some loving in the morning, mothers let them come into bed with them.'

A hand snaked around her waist and started tickling the squirming little body she was cuddling. 'Who's this in my bed?' Price growled, and lifted himself to poke his head over Elizabeth's shoulder, inadvertently—or deliberately—pressing his hard warmth full length against her, making her well aware that his desire for her was unabated.

'It's Miss... it's Elizabeth!' Ricky crowed delightedly.

'Hmmm...'

Price nuzzled her bare shoulder, making her quiver with excitement. She was suddenly certain that he had been bluffing sleep all throughout her conversation with Ricky. And she was somewhat shamed by the quickening response of her body to his—even as she held his son!

'... I think I like this arrangement. We'd better keep her here, Ricky,' he said teasingly, but with a definite undertone of seriousness.

'Yes! We've got to keep her, Daddy!' Ricky agreed whole-heartedly.

'Which means we'd better do what she tells us. And no slip-ups. It's Miss Kent at school. Right?'

'Right!' Ricky echoed gravely. 'I won't slip up, Daddy.'

'I know you won't, son. You're the best there is,' Price said with loving approval.

Ricky glowed.

'But we have got a problem,' Price added warningly. 'Elizabeth wasn't sure you'd want her to stay, so she didn't bring all her clothes and things with her. I'll have to take her home this morning to get ready for school. And time's ticking away. How about hopping downstairs and telling Lorna that Elizabeth is here and we'll want breakfast at seven o'clock? Give us time to get washed and dressed, and we'll be right down there with you.'

'OK!' Ricky scrambled out of the bed, then paused to give Elizabeth a big smile. 'This is the best morning I've ever had,' he declared, and skipped out of the room, obviously delighted with the prospect of spreading the good news.

'I'll second that,' Price murmured, nibbling Elizabeth's ear as he slid his hand down between her thighs and made her sensuously aware of all kinds of things. 'You handled Ricky beautifully. I'm in awe of your delicate sensibilities, and need—very urgently—to explore them further.'

He rolled her towards him and began kissing and caressing her breasts with a seductive expertise that rendered her totally incapable of battling the pleasure streaking through her. 'Price . . . there isn't time,' she said weakly.

'We'll have a fast shower—together,' he purred wickedly, and continued creating magical havoc inside her.

'Who. . . who. . . is. . . Lorna?' Elizabeth managed to ask, although it was terribly difficult to concentrate her mind on anything but what Price was doing to her.

'Runs house . . . no worry for you . . .'

'Price . . .' she moaned in a paroxysm of melting pleasure.

He took her swiftly and lifted her once more to sensational extremities of feeling. And when she was too limp and languorous to move, he carried her into an en suite bathroom, stood her under a warm shower, and soaped and washed her wildly sensitised body while she held up the thick mass of her hair—as he instructed—so that it wouldn't get wet.

By seven o'clock Elizabeth had managed to get herself looking reasonably respectable. But she knew that the glow on her skin wasn't entirely due to a sense of embarrassment as Price took her downstairs to the breakfast-room.

It was a bright, cosy room which led off the kitchen. Double glass doors faced on to a small courtyard which flourished with azaleas in magnificent bloom, providing a lovely cheerful view. However, Lee Briggs immediately blocked it, rising from his chair at the table, his homely face wreathed in a huge grin.

'Morning, Miss Kent. Sure is nice of you to join us.' He nodded approvingly at Price. 'A real good morning, Ricky reckons.'

'Yes. Thank you,' Elizabeth said in an agony of self-consciousness.

Ricky hopped off his chair to pull out the one next to him. 'Sit here beside me,' he appealed, looking up at her with shy adoration.

'Thank you, Ricky.'

Price saw her settled, then took the chair at the head of the table, a decidedly smug look on his face. He grinned at Elizabeth and said, 'A real good morning.'

She didn't know whether to squirm or laugh, but the intimate knowledge of her in those golden eyes sent a surge of heat around her blood. She was amazed at herself. For three years of married life she had dreaded having sex—tried to avoid it through one strategem or another, suffered it—and now Price had only to look at her... but with him it wasn't sex as she had known it. It was making love—even if it was only physical love.

But it surely had to be more than that?

It couldn't be this good if it wasn't more.

She felt... so complete with him.

Ricky poured her a glass of fresh orange juice from a jug. Price poured her coffee. Les offered her a plate of toast. All three of them made her feel like a queen to be pampered and cosseted.

Lorna Fulton swept through the kitchen doorway with a loaded tray of steaming hot bacon and eggs, took one look at the stars in the honest grey eyes of the teacher Ricky adored, and decided on the spot that Price had got himself a good woman. And he'd better marry her fast, or she would have something to say to him!

'Elizabeth, this is Lorna Fulton,' Price said smoothly, his mouth twitching at the arch look on Lorna's face. 'Elizabeth Kent, Lorna.'

'Very pleased to meet you, Miss Kent,' she beamed at Elizabeth as she unloaded the tray on to the table. 'Our boy here never stops talking about you. I'm afraid I'm too old to look like a mother to him, and it's about time Price took proper notice of the fact and did something about it.'

'I... I hope I'm not putting you out by being here, Mrs Fulton,' Elizabeth said in some confusion. The woman was not really old. She was a plump and well-worn fifty, exuding energy and good humour, but Elizabeth was not quite sure how she viewed the situation, although she sensed approval of herself.

'Not putting me out at all. Delighted to have you with us,' came the very positive reply. 'Now you help yourself to a good breakfast, dear, and I'll be even happier.' She shot Price a meaningful look and took herself back to the kitchen.

Elizabeth didn't usually eat a cooked breakfast, but she had an incredibly good appetite this morning. She did Lorna Fulton's cooking proud, which earned more approval.

Price used the mealtime to instruct Les Briggs that he was to pick up Elizabeth as well as Ricky after school, take her to her apartment, and both of them were to help pack whatever Elizabeth wanted to bring to the house. Lorna was informed that the study was to be prepared to accommodate Elizabeth's books and papers as well as his own, and the dressing-room off his bedroom was to be cleared of anything unnecessary in order to make room for Elizabeth's clothes.

Which was all extremely embarrassing for Elizabeth, but done with such smooth and authoritative efficiency that she didn't like to utter any protest. Besides, Price was only effecting what she had decided. But it felt so strange—her whole life being changed literally in front of her. It was both exciting and frightening.

And it was only when they had taken their leave of the others and Price was escorting her out to the triple garage that Elizabeth remembered that she had had second thoughts about her decision last night. If Price hadn't held her, kissed her, swept her upstairs with him—if she hadn't gone to sleep and woken up with Ricky looking at her—somehow it had all fallen out of her hands.

But she didn't regret it.

Yet...

She automatically baulked as Price opened the passenger door of the Jaguar sports car. Then, telling herself he had given her no reason to fear his driving, she pushed herself to settle on to the seat without uttering a word.

'I'll sell this and buy another kind of car, Elizabeth,' he said soothingly.

'No!' she cried in immediate protest, not wanting him to think she didn't trust him, and instinctively rebelling against any change in his nature for her sake. 'It's all right,' she assured him. 'You're not...' irony curved her mouth '...not stupid, Price.'

The tawny-yellow eyes danced with an appreciation that lifted her pulse-rate. 'Thank you,' he smiled, and quietly closed the door, shutting her in.

She didn't feel any panic or apprehension. But when he slid into the seat beside her and shut his door, she savoured the sense of togetherness that was instantly evoked by being alone with him.

'You mustn't worry about Les or Lorna, Elizabeth,' he said as he smoothly steered the car into the traffic running towards Chatswood. 'They've been with me for years and there's not a mean bone in their bodies. I know Les hardly looks genteel, but I'd trust him ahead of most people, and whatever I say goes with him. You can't buy that kind of loyalty, and I value it very highly.'

Elizabeth threw a questioning look at Price. 'He looks as though he was a fighter at some time.'

'He was,' Price nodded. 'He stepped into the ring once too often and suffered a certain amount of brain damage. Les is a legacy from my father, Elizabeth. He was down and out. Finished in the fighting game with nowhere to go. Dad took him in. Gave him a job as a kind of caretaker for his home. Les had been brought up in the concrete jungle of Redfern, and he loved Dad's garden. He was always out pottering around, fascinated with growing flowers. When Dad was killed, Les was utterly bereft . . . lost . . .'

'So you took him in,' Elizabeth said softly, her eyes shining with pleasure at Price's caring heart.

'Les earns his keep.'

Elizabeth smiled at the curt little justification. She was absolutely certain that Price would have taken Les in whether he earned his keep or not. But he had given the ex-fighter pride and dignity in entrusting Ricky to his care, and what she had seen of the garden clearly demonstrated the loving commitment of the man, however simple he might be.

'And how did you get Lorna?' she asked, wondering if there was another telling story behind the housekeeper's employment.

Price's mouth twitched with amusement. 'Lorna landed herself on me. She turned up on my doorstep when I brought Ricky home—after my father's death—and said I'd be needing a live-in housekeeper, and she'd do a better job for me than anyone else. She didn't exactly give me a choice. Just barged in and took over.'

His liking for her ran through the amusement, and Elizabeth knew that Lorna was another special person in his household. 'She must have known you beforehand—to turn up like that?' she prompted.

'Mmm . . . Lorna's husband was killed in a fall on the racetrack. He was a jockey. Dad helped her over the worst, until she got on her feet with a catering business. Then her only child—a teenage daughter—was involved in a car accident and became a paraplegic.'

'Oh, lord! How dreadful for her!' Elizabeth murmured in anguished sympathy.

'Yes. It was,' Price murmured with a heavy sigh. 'Lorna came to me. Asked me to argue her case in court for compensation—so that her daughter could get the best rehabilitation possible. I got that for her, but despite all Lorna's care the girl died a couple of years later of kidney failure. Lorna donated the rest of the compensation money to the care of the handicapped and went back to work. But she didn't have much heart in living any more.'

Price threw Elizabeth his crooked smile. 'I think she feels that Ricky and I are her mission in life now. Anyway, being our housekeeper has made her feel happy and useful. However, I should warn you—she's very forthright about having her say occasionally. Straight from the shoulder, Lorna is.'

His eyes twinkled at her. 'She thinks you're lovely. And I shouldn't be taking advantage of you. I'll get a flea in my ear if I do you wrong. So you have no reason not to be completely at ease with her. OK?'

'Yes,' she nodded, feeling even happier with the prospect of becoming one of Price's family. That was really what his household was—an adopted family. Except she wasn't a dependant or a child.

The thought suddenly reminded her of the issue that had brought her to Price last night. Ricky! And the school-board meeting! It had not been discussed at all. It had been completely thrown into abeyance by the resolution of their relationship. Yet the problem was critical—it was going to be decided today!

'Price!' she burst out anxiously. 'What are you going to do about Ricky and the school?'

There was an almost imperceptible tightening of his face. 'I'll settle it . . . one way or another,' he said flatly.

'But how?'

'Don't worry about it. There's nothing you can do, Elizabeth. Leave it to me.'

'I will worry. I can't help worrying. If they do that to Ricky, I'm going to resign,' she said fiercely.

'Let's hope it won't come to that,' Price muttered grimly.

'Is there any way you can prevent it?' Elizabeth cried.

Price didn't answer her.

With a sinking sense of desperation, Elizabeth realised that they were turning into her street. The trip home was almost over, and she didn't know what was on Price's mind—what he intended to do. And time was ticking away. She couldn't keep him with her or she would be late for school. But this was more important!

He pulled up outside her apartment-block, switched off the engine, undid his seat-belt and turned to her, his eyes glittering with a savage sense of purpose that belied the smile on his lips. 'I won't see you to your door, Elizabeth. It's best if I get to my office as soon as possible. But I need a booster for my confidence first.'

And before she could say a word he leaned over and kissed her with a hard, hungry passion that drove everything else into a limbo of weak formless things.

'Go with Les and Ricky after school,' he murmured, his mouth roving distractingly over her lips. 'I'll come home to you the moment I'm free.'

He moved abruptly away, got out of the car and swiftly rounded it to her side, opening her door for her. Elizabeth climbed out, her thoughts clicking raggedly into place again, her pulse racing in agitation.

'Price...isn't there anything I can do?' she asked anxiously.

He smiled, but his eyes were those of a tiger again. 'I think, perhaps, the gods may be on our side today,' he said, then touched her cheek in a farewell salute.

She stared after the car until it disappeared around the corner, her heart hammering in dismay. If Price was leaving the matter to luck—no, she didn't believe that. There had been that look in his eyes—the look of fighting to the death before he would ever knuckle under to prejudice and injustice.

The sheer animal savagery that had emanated from him last night sent a sudden chill through Elizabeth's mind as she recalled the words he had spoken—'No one attacks my son and gets away unscathed.'

But what could he do? How could he change the minds of the board members?

Then she remembered the way he had torn her to shreds that day at the court-house—the dark bitter side of him that wanted to wound as he had been wounded. He had shown her the soft, humane side of him this morning. Perhaps it was the mix of the two that made him such an enthralling lover. But it would be stupid of her ever to forget that dangerous quality which could lash out at any moment. And hurt.

But hurting people wouldn't help Ricky in the long run. It only created more ill will. Surely Price must realise that? If only she hadn't been so distracted by what was happening to her—if only there had been more time to talk. Or had Price deliberately kept her mind on other things—sharing the good, but still not prepared to share the bad?

Elizabeth tried to push her anxiety aside as she trudged up the stairs to her apartment. One thing was certain, anyway. If those board members expelled Ricky from the school, this would be her last day at Alpha Academy, too. And she would make it all up to Ricky by being the mother he wanted. As best she could.

As for Price—Elizabeth didn't have any definite answers. All she knew was that she wanted to be with him. Even at the risk of getting hurt.

CHAPTER TWELVE

ELIZABETH found it extremely difficult to keep her mind concentrated on teaching. Not only did she worry about the board meeting, but having Ricky in her class was a constant distraction. He faithfully called her Miss Kent, but the sherry-brown eyes kept dancing at her with the secret knowledge they shared. Although she didn't mind that. Not at all. It was very heart-warming. But it did set her thoughts wandering when she was supposed to be giving lessons.

Nor was there any relaxation for her at lunchtime. The afternoon meeting of the school-board was the main buzz of conversation in the staff-room. Speculation was rife as to why it had been called, and what new decisions were about to be made. Elizabeth was too distressed about it to enlighten them on the issue which most concerned her.

She kept remembering what Price had said last night—'I wouldn't have even bothered to use their kind of dirt...but I'll use it now.' And that worried her to the depths of her soul. Two wrongs didn't make a right. Her initial mistake with Price had taught her that. Very forcefully. And she didn't want him making an even worse mistake.

If he stooped to blackmail—if he hurt people really badly—how could she live with that? What was justified and what wasn't? Ricky's expulsion certainly wasn't, but how far would Price go to prevent it? She desperately prayed that he would stay on the right side of the law. As his father had wanted. As she wanted.

Mr Fairchild did not seek her out to ask any questions, directly or indirectly, and since she had nothing constructive to say to him—beyond what had been said yesterday—there was no point in her seeking him out.

The afternoon dragged by. It was sheer torture not to know what was happening over in the boardroom. When the last school-bell rang to signal the end of lessons for the day, Elizabeth could not bear to remain in ignorance any longer. She had to see the headmaster. And if the worst had happened, she would hand him her resignation, effective immediately.

She called Ricky to her side as the other children trooped out of the classroom. He came with a happy skip of anticipation and Elizabeth's heart bled for the crimes committed against innocents.

'Ricky, I have to go and see the headmaster before I leave school today. Could you and Les wait for me in the car? I won't be too long,' she promised. 'Maybe twenty minutes. Will that be all right?'

'We can easily wait that long,' he assured her. 'We'll play I-spy until you come.'

'I-spy?' she quizzed, worried that he might get into trouble around the playground.

He grinned. 'You know. I spy with my little eye, something starting with a letter of the alphabet. Les and I always play that when we have to wait in the car.'

'Oh!' Elizabeth smiled in relief. 'That's fine, then. Off you go, now.'

He ran off with unbounded joy in the future that lay ahead of him. Elizabeth paused only long enough to remove the tiger cowrie shell from the back of her desk-drawer and place it safely at the bottom of her handbag. She had promised Ricky she would keep it. And she always would, come what may.

Only teachers' cars stood in the private parking area near the administration centre, so Elizabeth deduced that the board meeting was definitely over. Which meant the headmaster should be in his office. Elizabeth screwed up her courage and knocked firmly on his door.

There was no answer.

She took a deep breath. If Mr Fairchild was there and didn't want to be interrupted—too bad! She opened the door.

He was there, all right! His back was turned to her, and he was standing at the bay window behind his desk, shaking his head at something.

'Mr Fairchild?' Elizabeth said somewhat aggressively, too churned up to employ any subtlety in her approach.

He swung around, obviously startled by her presence. He must have been deep in thought if he hadn't heard her come in, Elizabeth decided, and her heart sank a little lower as she pessimistically surmised what was occupying his mind.

'Ah . . . Miss Kent,' he muttered distractedly. 'Good of you to come by. I've—er—finished with Richard Domenico's class records. You can collect them.'

The blood drained from Elizabeth's face. 'You mean . . . they did expel him?'

He looked up sharply, really focusing on her for the first time. A funny little smile curled his mouth. 'On the contrary. I'm not quite sure if we've just had a coup or a revolution.' He shook his head again and waved her to a chair. 'Maybe you can explain it to me, Miss Kent.'

Coup? Revolution? Confusion rattled through the surge of relief at Ricky's reprieve. Her mind finally clutched what was implied in the headmaster's words. Some violence had been done to someone! Her fears about Price's intervention redoubled, and her legs felt wobbly as she moved to the chair. She was grateful to sink on to it.

Mr Fairchild settled himself on his throne and looked at her with an odd expression of bemusement.

'Extraordinary man, Price Domenico,' he said, half to himself it seemed. 'Of course, I knew he was brilliant, but if anyone had told me what was to occur in that board meeting this afternoon, I wouldn't have believed it.'

Tell me! Elizabeth's mind shrieked, but she could not bring herself to voice the words. She stared at Mr Fairchild, desperately willing him to exonerate Price of any wrongdoing.

His eyes glazed with wonder and incredulity. 'A mauling with blood and guts—that I would have believed.' Again he shook his head. 'But the finesse of the man . . . the diplomacy . . .'

Elizabeth took a deep breath, but even so her voice shook as she tried to press the headmaster into hard facts instead of disconnected comment.

'Mr Fairchild, are you saying that Price was there? At the meeting?'

'Yes.' A weird little cackle erupted from the usually honeyed chords of the headmaster's throat. It sent shivers down Elizabeth's spine. But his next words shot any train of thought to pieces. 'Price Domenico came with Mrs Wetherington-Jones. At her invitation.'

'Mrs Wetherington-Jones?'

'The same!' the headmaster nodded, in complete empathy with Elizabeth's shock. 'She proceeded to resign from the board and nominated Price Domenico to take her place. She dumbfounded everyone by giving a very persuasive speech about his many qualifications, and the vote was carried forthwith.'

'Price is on the board?' Elizabeth squeaked.

'He very graciously accepted the position,' the headmaster confirmed with another little cackle.

Elizabeth could not feel amused. The question pummelling her heart was, how had Price done it? She swallowed hard and forced herself to probe for answers, however unpalatable they might be. She had to know.

'Mr Fairchild, did Mrs Wetherington-Jones look upset? Or seem frightened?'

The headmaster shook his head. 'That was the extraordinary thing. Not a sign of any threat being held over her head. She sounded totally genuine in everything she said about Price Domenico, and looked relieved and pleased when everyone accepted her word. She even smiled at him.'

Elizabeth shook her head. The whole thing was unanswerable. Mrs Wetherington-Jones was no actress. Everything she thought and felt showed on her face. How Price had achieved such a turnabout in her attitude towards him was completely beyond Elizabeth.

'And then...' the headmaster continued, warming to the incredible aspects of the story '...Price Domenico lauded Mrs Wetherington-Jones for all the fine work she had done for the benefit of Alpha Academy. He followed this with a splendid exposition of sweet-talking the other members about their unselfish generosity of spirit in shouldering responsibilities for the good of the community at large. And having prepared the way so skilfully for the one bitter pill...'

The headmaster paused for breath.

Elizabeth was holding hers.

'...he pointed out—as an expert on the law—that there were some anomalies in our constitution that really should be corrected forthwith. In fact, for the protection of the good name and reputation of Alpha Academy, the matter was urgent. Any decisions made could not carry the ratification of the law if challenged. The board immediately voted that Price Domenico should amend the constitution as he saw fit—as an expert on the law. And the meeting was adjourned.'

He raised his hands in a throw-away gesture. 'Needless to say, Richard Domenico's name was not mentioned by anyone. And please don't ask me how or why all this came about, Miss Kent—but it seems we have peace in our time. For some considerable time to come. We may even be able to keep to our high goals. The pursuit of excellence...' He nodded solemnly. 'I saw it today...yes, I saw it today. Excellence! A very dangerous man, Price Domenico. Unstoppable when he's got the bit between the teeth.'

Elizabeth shook her head dazedly. Dangerous, unstoppable—she had to agree with that, but he hadn't done anything wrong. He couldn't have. Whatever Price had done, it had to be good, not bad, or he couldn't have achieved these results. A deep, warm pleasure bubbled over the fading residue of fear.

'He was so right!' the headmaster said admiringly. 'The touch of a master politician. He even sounded moral.'

'I believe he is, Mr Fairchild,' Elizabeth said, rising to her feet. 'In fact, from my point of view, Price Domenico is the most moral man I've ever known. And I think he'll be a splendid addition to the school-board.'

She stepped forward and lifted the folder of Ricky's class records from his desk, hugging them to her in uninhibited joy. 'I have to be getting on my way now. Thank you for seeing me, Mr Fairchild.'

He suddenly recollected himself and rose to his feet in a burst of agitation as Elizabeth headed towards his door. 'Miss Kent! I...er...'

She looked enquiringly at him, noting a dark tide of blood creeping up his neck.

'This conversation...you realise it is completely confidential. You were—er—conversant with the problem, and I appreciated your...your special interest.'

'Of course, Mr Fairchild,' Elizabeth assured him brightly. 'But you will be announcing the new member of the school-board to the staff, and you'll say all the good things about Price Domenico, won't you?'

'Certainly! Perfectly justified. Can only do good for Alpha Academy.'

Elizabeth bestowed a brilliant smile on him. 'I knew you would say that, Mr Fairchild. And you're absolutely right. You have my full support and confidence.'

He beamed at her, and Elizabeth quickly slipped out of the office while the going was good.

She wanted to laugh and shout for joy, and she only just managed to keep her walk to a lilting prance. The temptation to run and skip and leap around like Ricky was almost overwhelming, but her ingrained sense of dignity wouldn't allow it. However, she couldn't bear the delay of taking Ricky's records back to the classroom. She made straight for the school gate, every step a song of exultation.

Price hadn't slain the dragons at all! He had co-opted them to his purpose. How he had done it she had no idea, but she would get it all out of him tonight. He couldn't possibly hold out on her. She would grill him unmercifully. And kiss him in between. She wasn't above a little feminine persuasion when need and inclination demanded it.

Ricky and Les were waiting in the silver Mercedes she had seen beside Price's Jaguar in the garage this morning. Ricky spotted her coming and opened the door, leaping out in his eagerness to usher her into the car. Elizabeth couldn't contain her elation a moment longer. She tossed the folder and her handbag on to the back seat, picked up Ricky and whirled him around before hugging him to her.

'Your father, Ricky Domenico, is the most wonderful man in the world!' she told him, bubbling with happiness, then carried him into the car and shut the door on Alpha Academy, thrilled out of her mind with her new private world.

'That he is,' said Les, in grinning agreement. 'Price is just like Joe, Miss Kent. A better man there never was. And Price is the same. You'll be real happy with him and Ricky.'

'Come on, Les,' Ricky urged excitedly. 'We've got to get all Elizabeth's things so she'll stay with us forever and ever.'

'Right you are, Ricky!' Les said with enthusiasm. 'Got to get those things. No reason not to stay with us then.'

Elizabeth laughed. She had the delicious sensation that they would both hijack her if she even looked like hesitating over coming home with them, and it was marvellous to feel wanted—really wanted and valued and loved. She wasn't quite sure if Price loved her, but Ricky certainly did. And she was getting more and more sure about her feelings for both father and son.

Les had stacked boxes in the boot of the car and they all carried them up the stairs to her apartment in a kind of triumphant procession. The packing didn't take long. Elizabeth didn't know what she should do about her furniture. The electric typewriter certainly had to come with her, and Les reckoned the television and video sets shouldn't be left behind, but eventually they locked the door on the rest—to be collected or disposed of some other time.

No one suggested that Elizabeth might ever be returning to live in the apartment. She shied away from any such thought herself. Her commitment to Price was very close to rock-solid, even though they hadn't known each other very long. Somehow time didn't seem to be terribly relevant. It was a matter of rightness, and nothing had felt more right in Elizabeth's whole life.

Mrs Fulton—Lorna, as she insisted on being called—had all the space organised for Elizabeth to settle into Price's home as if she had always belonged there. And she refused point-blank when Elizabeth offered to help her with preparing dinner.

'You teach all day, and then study for a university degree at night. You need some time off,' Lorna argued. 'You just relax, now, and let me look after things. We've all got our jobs, and that's how things work here. No call for you to be doing household chores. Though you can tell me if there's anything you'd like special for meals and snacks. I'll get it in or cook it for you.'

'I think you're going to spoil me, Lorna,' Elizabeth laughed.

'Well, a little bit of spoiling doesn't go astray,' the housekeeper smiled, then added archly, 'Price is a good man, you know. You couldn't do better.'

And having planted what she hoped was a very fertile seed, Lorna swept off to the kitchen to cook a meal that was worthy of this auspicious occasion. She sent Les out to pick a bunch of his best flowers, and set the dining-room table with what she considered to be the most romantic tableware. Only two places were laid. Ricky always had an early tea, and she and Les would eat in the breakfast-room.

Lorna's parting words did bear fruit as Elizabeth unpacked her clothes and hung them up. But not quite the fruit that the housekeeper wanted. The wonderful sense of euphoria that had begun in the headmaster's office slowly drained away with the entry of more serious thoughts about her future.

She had no quarrel with Lorna's judgement of Price's character. Quite apart from her strong feelings about him, all the evidence pointed to Price being a man whose word could be trusted. And she wasn't really against marriage as such, but she didn't want to make another bad mistake. On the other hand, if Price ever asked her to marry him—and if she did marry him—Elizabeth didn't believe he would turn into a tyrant. He was essentially fair and generous.

And brilliant!

The manoeuvring he had done today was testament enough of that. Even the headmaster had more or less acknowledged that Price had left him completely floundering. And everyone else!

The only thing was, Price hadn't seen fit to confide his plan to her. Where she was concerned, it seemed he only had one thing on his mind. And how long did desire last, if he couldn't share his thoughts with her?

She heaved a sigh, wishing she knew more about the woman he had married. Had Rosalie been brilliant, too? While Elizabeth had proved to herself that she was certainly not stupid, she wasn't sure that Price would not get bored with her after a while. She was hardly in his class when it came to brains.

And if he got bored and irritated with her...

But then there was Ricky. And she yearned to have some children of her own as well—with Price as their father. She suddenly remembered that she hadn't thought of precautions last night, either, but a moment's consideration assured her she had almost certainly been safe from falling pregnant again. All the same, she couldn't keep on in this careless way, not now she was living with Price. He would certainly want some say in the matter. Would he like to have more children... with her?

It was too soon to be thinking such things, Elizabeth chided herself. But she could hardly help it when she went downstairs to the family-room where Ricky was watching television, and he climbed on her lap the moment she sat down with him. He had been bathed and dressed in his pyjamas and he smelled of baby powder. She couldn't resist dropping a kiss on his forehead, and Ricky reached up and pressed a quick, shy kiss on her cheek.

'I love having you here, Elizabeth,' he said artlessly, snuggling closer to her.

She hugged him and brushed her cheek over his soft black curls. 'I love it, too,' she whispered. And the warm melting feeling was shining in her eyes when she looked up and found Price in the doorway, watching them.

'Hello,' he said quietly, and there was something in the tone of his voice that mirrored the warm liquid gold of his eyes.

'Daddy!' Ricky was off Elizabeth's lap and throwing himself at his father in the twinkling of an eye, and Price hoisted him up to his shoulder in exuberant response.

'Les and I got it all worked out while Elizabeth was seeing the headmaster this afternoon,' Ricky prattled excitedly.

Price grinned at Elizabeth and held out his free hand to her. 'Saw the headmaster, did you?'

'Yes,' she said, rising to her feet and curling her fingers around his. He squeezed them tight, and again she felt the magic sense of togetherness that dimmed all her doubts. Whatever else happened in the future, she was glad she had come to live with him. At least she would always have this to remember.

'And what did you and Les work out, Ricky?' Price asked his son indulgently.

'All you've got to do is marry Elizabeth...' the sherry-brown eyes shot her a yearning look '...and then I can call her Mummy.'

'That's true,' Price agreed, without batting an eyelid, while Elizabeth's heart started performing aerobics. 'But I've got one problem, son. I've got to convince Elizabeth that I'm the man she wants to marry. And that might take a little time.'

It was a deft postponement of the issue. Elizabeth was intensely grateful for it. She had certainly not foreseen this kind of pressure from Ricky, and it was disturbing. Had she done the right thing in coming to live with Price? By the same reasoning she had used for herself, surely it was better for Ricky to have some mother-love than none at all? But the little boy's next words completely floored her.

'No, it won't, Daddy,' Ricky assured him. 'Elizabeth loves living here with us. And she said you were the most wonderful man in the world.'

Elizabeth blushed to the roots of her hair and didn't know where to look. She could hardly blame Ricky for repeating her own words, yet they sounded so compromising. And put both Price and her right on the spot! She was mortified by her careless indiscretion.

'Did she now?' Price said in a tone of warm interest. 'Well, that sounds pretty good, Ricky. But we mustn't push Elizabeth until she's ready. Getting married is a big decision. Let's just be happy that she's here with us. All right?'

Ricky heaved an impatient sigh. 'All right,' he dragged out.

On the one thin level where her mind was still working, Elizabeth had to admire Price's handling of the situation. But then—if he could handle Mrs Wetherington-Jones and a school-board of hard-nosed members, the side-tracking of a little boy's disgruntlement was certainly child's play to him.

He started a light-hearted barrage of questions about the afternoon's moving operation, which Ricky happily answered as they all settled back in front of the television. Elizabeth could not bring herself to take part in the conversation, but she forced a smile occasionally. At Ricky.

Gradually her embarrassment diminished, and she grew aware of Price's hand still holding hers. It was comforting, but it didn't answer the problem Ricky had posed. She had no doubt that the little boy would return to it sooner or later. And then what?

CHAPTER THIRTEEN

ELIZABETH had barely recovered her composure by Ricky's bedtime, and it did not help matters when he insisted that she, as well as his father, had to tuck him into bed. Not that Elizabeth had any objection to doing so, but as they settled Ricky for the night Price kept darting glances at her—warm, speculative glances that suggested he was not averse to Ricky's suggestion of marriage... if she wasn't averse to it.

It threw Elizabeth into further confusion. She did not want Price asking her to marry him for his son's sake—to provide a mother. Only if he truly wanted her as his wife. And even then she wasn't sure she could accept.

The moment the door had been closed on Ricky, Price caught her to him in a very possessive embrace. 'The most wonderful man in the world?' he teased.

Elizabeth gave a self-conscious laugh. 'You know why I said that. How did you do it, Price?'

He grinned. 'I thought of you.'

Then his mouth claimed hers with a sweet hunger that devoured the possibility of any more words. And Elizabeth melted against him, uncaring of anything but the delicious pleasure of kissing him back with all her heart and body and soul.

'Elizabeth...' he groaned, his hands almost kneading her body in the urgency of his desire. He dragged in a deep breath and managed a crooked smile. 'Much as I want to make mad, passionate love to you, Lorna will never forgive me if we keep her special dinner waiting. I saw the dining-room as I came in. She's got everything laid on good and proper. I just hope she's stopped short of having a shotgun handy.' He gave a soft chuckle. 'If you're not already aware, there's a conspiracy afoot to get us married. And you can't blame me. It's all your fault.'

He was making a joke out of it, trying to ease the awkwardness she had felt. She understood and appreciated his attempt to lighten any pressure that had been laid on her, but it was surprisingly difficult to answer in a similarly light vein.

'How can you say that?' she protested, anxious to establish her innocence. 'I haven't——'

Price gently touched his fingers to her lips and his smile denied any fault in her. 'I did tell you you're beautiful. With a very sweet nature to match. The conclusion is inevitable, my love. I'd be a fool to let you get away.'

Elizabeth made no protest as he tucked her arm around his and walked her downstairs. Price had called her *my love*. It might not mean precisely what she would like it to mean, but that argument didn't stop her from feeling as if she were floating on air.

Either Lorna had a good ear or she had kept an eagle eye on the dining-room doorway. The moment Elizabeth and Price sat down at the table, she was in to serve a starter of fish and asparagus topped with hollandaise sauce. Les trailed after her with a bottle of champagne. He poured it into beautiful fluted Baccarat glasses. His Cheshire cat grin was wider than ever.

Price gravely thanked them, but his eyes danced at Elizabeth in secret amusement. Which brought her slightly more down to earth. Love might be one thing, but neither he nor she was going to be rushed into marriage by anyone else, however well-intended their wishes were.

Nevertheless, she was extraordinarily happy just to be with him, and as she expressed her own appreciation to Les and Lorna for their kind attentions her face glowed with such luminous beauty that they swiftly departed to let things develop as they should. If Price and Elizabeth had any sense of co-operation at all.

Elizabeth immediately seized the opportunity to have her curiosity about the board meeting satisfied. She insisted Price give her an explanation of how he had managed everything—particularly Mrs Wetherington-Jones!

'She's part-owner of a brothel,' he said, absolutely dead-pan.

Elizabeth almost choked on her fish. 'Mrs Wetherington-Jones?'

'She didn't know about it. I suspected she didn't. A nice little tax-scam for her husband. She simply signed papers he gave her to sign. It was hidden behind a company name. It turned up in our investigation for Andrew Hartley. But Wetherington-Jones wasn't the big fish we were after. He was simply a minnow on the edge of the tide. The information was immaterial to the defence, but I didn't mention that to Mrs Wetherington-Jones.'

Elizabeth looked at him unbelievingly. 'What did you say to her?'

His mouth twisted in irony. 'I could have used it as a club over her head. Subpoenaed her into court. Splashed it all over the Sunday newspapers. I might have done it—but for you.'

The look in his eyes did nothing to help Elizabeth's digestion. She swallowed hard and managed to ask, 'What did I have to do with it?'

'Elizabeth.' He shook his head in indulgent bemusement at her innocence, then tried to explain how deeply she had touched his conscience and his soul.

'All these years I've been carrying an aggressive chip on my shoulder—too proud to make any explanations of myself or my father. A kind of perverse snobbery, if you like. And probably just as prejudiced in its way as the Wetherington-Jones type of snobbery. You showed me that, Elizabeth. You taught me that people should be given a better chance than I was giving them. To reach out rather than knock away. Even if you get rejected, it's still better to offer the truth than not to try.'

Pleasure rippled through her, bringing a luminous glow to her eyes. Price found it difficult to concentrate his mind on what he had to say, but he pushed himself on.

'So I went to Mrs Wetherington-Jones this morning. She was totally shocked and distressed by what I had to tell her. As I suspected, she was completely ignorant of her connection with a brothel. I assured her that I wasn't in the business of destroying people or their reputations, unless it was absolutely necessary for the cause of justice. I would do my best to protect her good name but, for her own sake, she should get her house in order as soon as possible.'

Price sighed as he remembered the scene. 'She was pathetically grateful for my discretion. I actually did feel sorry for her. And, to her credit, I didn't have to prompt her about Ricky. She poured it all out and pleaded for me to tell her how she could make amends. I expressed a wish that next time there was a vacancy on the school-board, I would appreciate her support for nomination, if she felt she could bring herself to do that.'

A wry smile curved his lips. 'I'll say this for Mrs Wetherington-Jones—when she takes up a cause, she gives her whole heart to it. I have to respect that in the woman. Nothing would do but I join the board this very day and set everything to rights. By the time we parted this afternoon, we were at least allies, if not friends. And no harm can ever come to Ricky at Alpha Academy.'

'I was right,' Elizabeth breathed happily. 'You *are* the most wonderful man in the world, Price Domenico. And I'm so glad you didn't club Mrs Wetherington-Jones over the head. Although I've never liked her, I can imagine how destroyed the poor woman must have felt when you told her about the brothel.'

'It certainly made her more sympathetic to me and mine,' Price said drily. 'And that, my darling, was the major point. With you at my side, I intend to follow through on my father's ambition. And if I don't quite make it as a pillar of society, it won't be for the want of judicious effort.'

Elizabeth flushed. 'I'm not society, Price. I'm just an ordinary——'

'You are not ordinary, Elizabeth Mary Alexandra Kent,' he corrected her emphatically. He lifted his glass of champagne in a toast to her. 'You're extremely extraordinary. In fact, quite brilliant. And I won't hear anything to the contrary.'

The compliment was sweet to her ears—until he added the 'quite brilliant' part. Then a jab of uncertainty clouded her happiness. She almost wished Price wasn't so clever, but then he wouldn't be what he was. And the inescapable truth was that she could never match him. She could satisfy him in bed, be a mother to Ricky, but . . .

Price saw the shadow flit over her eyes and wondered what he had said wrong. It was so imperative he get everything right, and somehow he had blundered. His mind skated quickly over all she had told him about her life—the father who had been too blindly bigoted to see her worth, the husband who had almost destroyed her—and he could find no clue to what she was thinking.

Lorna came in to whip away the plates and serve the main meal. Elizabeth roused herself to compliment the housekeeper on her cooking. Price thought hard. He had to draw that shadow from her mind.

The moment Lorna left he smiled and said, 'I take it you didn't hand in your resignation when you saw the headmaster this afternoon?'

She relaxed and laughed. 'No, I didn't. Not after he told me what happened at the meeting. He's very happy at the way things turned out. He thought you were brilliant.'

The twinkle faded from her eyes as she spoke those last words, and she picked up her knife and fork and started attacking the meal.

Brilliant... *stupid*—the connection clicked. And his heart bled for the damage that had been done to her over all those soul-destroying years. And it was so wrong! He had to make her see that it was wrong.

'Elizabeth,' he said softly.

She looked up. The open vulnerability in her eyes made his stomach churn. But she had to recognise the truth. With all the intensity of feeling inside him he willed her to see and believe.

'It took you to show me how wrong I've been—to tame the savage beast in me and make me see a better way of dealing with people. If anyone is brilliant, it's you.'

She smiled, but the smile didn't quite infiltrate her eyes. She put down her knife and fork, reached for her glass, sipped the champagne as if she was having difficulty in swallowing, then put the glass down again. She seemed to come to a decision. An inner tension tightened her face as she turned to him.

'I'm not in your class, Price,' she said flatly. 'You know I'm not. I get along all right with a lot of application, but...'

His hand reached across the table and took hers, pressing a warm reassurance. 'Elizabeth, please don't ever put yourself down. Not ever again. I might be able to do something faster than you, or remember things I've read more easily, but that's simply an ability I was born with. You have different talents. And much better ones, at that.'

Her head jerked away in automatic rejection, a grimace of disbelief distorting her lovely mouth.

'Elizabeth, look at me! Listen to me.'

The urgency in his voice dragged her eyes back to his, and he spoke with all the passionate conviction in his soul.

'You have a gift for rightness. And for loving. Those are the gifts that I want to spend a lifetime with. To me they are more special than anything else you could do.'

The golden eyes burned with a compelling, mesmerising light that spread a wonderful glow through Elizabeth. It was true—what he said. She was sure of it.

'You do realise, at this point, I must ask you to marry me,' he said with slow and very purposeful deliberation. 'It is your prerogative to say no. But I feel I should warn you of the consequences. I shall keep asking you and pursuing you for the next twenty or thirty years, or however long it takes to win your acceptance.'

Elizabeth was hopelessly tongue-tied, her emotions too strongly engaged for any speech.

Price drew in a deep breath, his eyes glittering with feverish need. 'I want you to say yes, Elizabeth. I want that more desperately than I've wanted anything in my life.'

Everything within Elizabeth yearned to say yes. But there were several things that needed to be known. She was committing herself again, after she had vowed to be free for the rest of her life. The contract she was entering into with this barrister was going to be very, very binding.

'Would I . . . would I ever take Rosalie's place in your heart, Price?'

'No,' he said sharply, his voice gathering a desperate edge as he plunged on. 'You take a place of your own, Elizabeth. A much larger, richer place. And I do not demean Rosalie's memory in any way when I say that. I loved her. But it was a young, inexperienced love that didn't know the depths of what could be shared. I would have cherished Rosalie as my wife all my life, because it's not in me to be unfaithful to a promise, once given. But circumstances ruled otherwise. And now I've met you . . .' his eyes burned into hers, determined on searing away any doubts she still harboured '. . . and you are the future, Elizabeth. Loyal friend, companion, partner, lover—you are all those things and more to me. To say that I love you does not say enough. I hoped that to say "Will you marry me?" might express it better.'

Tears of blissful joy welled into Elizabeth's eyes. 'Yes . . . yes, it does. And I will. I want to . . . very much . . .'

She was lifted out of her chair and wrapped in an embrace that barely gave her time to add, 'I love you,' before Price was stealing the words from her lips, tasting them, savouring them, and they were the sweetest honey in the world to him. The desire he had been repressing all evening could not be held back any longer.

'Let's go upstairs,' he murmured huskily.

Even though it was what she most wanted, too, Elizabeth felt guilty about leaving the meal that had been so especially prepared for them. 'The dinner . . . Lorna . . . she won't forgive us if we don't eat it.'

'Yes, she will!'

Price whipped a pen out of his pocket, spread his serviette out on the table and scrawled some words on it. Then he hugged Elizabeth to his side and swept her towards the door, barely giving her time to see what he had written.

The huge printed letters simply read, 'SHE SAID YES!'

CHAPTER FOURTEEN

It was the first Saturday after Easter—Graduation Day at the University of New England. The lawn outside the main administrative centre was manicured perfection. The surrounding trees were dressed in magnificent autumn hues: acid-yellow, burnt-orange, burgundy and deepest purple. The sun glittered through the leaves. It was a beautiful, crystal-clear morning—perfect for the ceremony which was being held in this open-air amphitheatre.

A canopied stage had been set up on the lower section of the lawn. There, garbed in all the imposing robes of their offices, were gathered the chancellor of the university, the bishop of Armidale, the heads of each faculty—joined this day to honour and congratulate academic achievement.

To one side of the stage sat the rows of students who had earned the highest degrees—masters and doctorates—among them academics from overseas with their richly coloured gowns and head-dresses denoting their origins—Oxford, Cambridge, Edinburgh. On the other side were the more sombre rows of those about to receive their bachelor degrees—all wearing the traditional black gowns and mortar-boards. Facing the stage, and set back in the shade of the towering pine trees, were the rows of chairs provided for visitors.

The dissertation on education had been given. The bishop had made his speech. The roll of names were being called one by one.

'Elizabeth Domenico...'

Her heart leapt with nervous excitement.

She stood up.

A high little voice piped over the crowd. 'That's my mummy!'

She saw Price hush Ricky and sit him on his knee. Their faces were wreathed in happy smiles. Les and Lorna looked as if they were bursting with pride and pleasure in her. Elizabeth managed to make it out to the aisle without tripping over any feet.

She lifted her chin. The mortar-board cap sat snugly on her head. A light breeze wafted the rippling mass of hair over her shoulders. The voluminous black gown didn't quite hide the fact that she was six months pregnant, but Elizabeth wasn't the least bit concerned about that. Her eyes were shining with dreams fulfilled. She walked down to the stage in grace and dignity and beauty.

The chancellor smiled at her as she gave him the ceremonial bow. He handed her the green folder tied in gold—the folder which held the long-coveted document which proved she wasn't stupid. Not that she needed it now. Not to prove anything. But somehow it seemed like a symbol of love and trust and respect—the whole sum of her relationship with her husband...and their family.

They wanted her to have it. They had encouraged and supported her ambition. They had come to see her receive her just reward. And celebrate all that she was.

Her hands trembled a little, but she forced them to take a firm hold of her Bachelor of Arts Degree.

'You mustn't give up now, Mrs Domenico,' the chancellor said indulgently. 'Not even with having a baby to take care of. Remember, constant learning is the art of life.'

'Yes,' she smiled. 'Thank you.'

Yes, she thought. She would study law next. Not that she wanted a career in it. Just so she could understand more of Price's work. Price didn't need professional help. He had taken on Andrew Hartley as a partner in his law practice after the ex-politician had been completely exonerated of all charges.

And she didn't want to go back to teaching, even though Mr Fairchild had assured her there would be a position for her at Alpha Academy if she changed her mind. She simply wanted to raise a family with the man she loved, and teaching their children to love and to appreciate learning was a fine enough career for her.

She turned away from the stage to walk back to her seat. Her eyes automatically sought Price in the front row of the visitor's section. He raised his hand in salute to her and she felt bathed in his love.

Yes, she thought. It had been so right to say yes to Price. Yes to trying; yes to trusting; yes to loving; yes to the faith in their future together; yes to a happiness that could not have been if she had not had the courage of her convictions.

She was not stupid.

Deep down within herself, Elizabeth had never believed she was, no matter what anyone else said.

She had clung—desperately at times—to her own self-esteem. But now, as her eyes clung to the tawny-gold eyes that held her in the highest esteem she could ever wish to attain, Elizabeth knew a fulfilment that filled her heart and overflowed into tears of overwhelming emotion.

Whatever anyone else thought simply didn't matter.

She had won the love of the most wonderful man in the world. And she returned his salute. With all her love for him.

2 NEW TITLES
FOR MARCH 1990

Jo *by Tracy Hughes.*
Book two in the sensational quartet of sisters in search of love…

In her latest cause, Jo's fiery nature helps her as an idealistic campaigner against the corrupting influence of the rock music industry. Until she meets the industry's heartbreaker, E. Z. Ellis, whose lyrics force her to think twice. £2.99

Sally Bradford's debut novel **The Arrangement** is a poignant romance that will appeal to readers everywhere.

Lawyer, Juliet Cavanagh, wanted a child, but not the complications of a marriage. Brady Talcott answered her advertisement for a prospective father, but he had conditions of his own… £2.99

WORLDWIDE

Available from Boots, Martins, John Menzies, W.H. Smith, Woolworths and other paperback stockists.